THE HOOK-UP EXPERIMENT

EMMA HART

NEW YORK TIMES BESTSELLING AUTHOR

THE HOOK-UP EXPERIMENT

Cover Design and Formatting by Emma Hart
Editing by Ellie at LoveNBooks

For my son.
The ever-present inspiration for my fictional kids.
Thanks for letting me borrow part of your breakfast obsession for Briony, little guy.

CHAPTER ONE

PEYTON

Brothers are assholes. And I'm still waiting for algebra to help me with my taxes.

THE DICK PICS WERE ENDLESS.

Six inches.

Four inches.

Eight inches.

Three inches plus Photoshop.

Really, they were all the same.

And it was a miracle if any of the men they were attached to were able to combine the size of the prize with the motion of the ocean.

In fact, the only difference in the dicks was where the owner of it wanted to put it. A mouth, a vagina, a butt... Another man's butt.

Those were my favorite types of matches to make. Good dicks were hard to find for women and for men—and sometimes, I matched more than just a hook-up for the gay population of New Orleans.

No wonder my brother fucking hated my business model. I had two gay weddings, one adoption, two proposals, and four long-term relationships under my belt. Not to mention a host of fuck-buddies.

He had one relationship and two break-ups.

Not that I was surprised, but orgasms clearly outweighed the whole getting-to-know each other stage.

I mean, seriously. There's not much more intimate than your cock inside someone else's ass.

Not that I'd know. The only cocks I owned came with batteries and lived in my drawer.

Or that I'd ever put anyone's cock up my ass...

I shook off the thought of anyone entering my exit. That was not a thought anyone needed to have while at their grandma's house for dinner.

I moved the guy whose profile was in front of me to a 'maybe' section. The girl I was hooking up was particular about what she wanted, and that only served to make my life easier.

You wouldn't tell your hairdresser she could color your hair whatever if you wanted to be blonde, would you?

I clicked onto the next profile as Ed Sheeran began crooning through my headphones. Shifting on the sofa, I swung my legs up onto another cushion and repositioned myself to where I could see if Mimi was coming back in from the kitchen.

She might have been accepting of what I did, but that didn't mean she wanted to be a part of the selection process.

The next profile loaded. He'd attached several pictures of himself, but I read through the submission first. Just out of a long-term relationship, looking for a feel-good fling...

We were onto something for my little red-headed friend.

Happy with the rest of his profile, I clicked on the attached photos. The first was of his face.

Handsome. Dark-haired. Exactly what she was looking for.

Next up: His body.

I let out a low whistle. Abs for days. Shoulders that gave away his strength.

Next up: The peen.

Oh, damn.

I loved it when people followed instructions—and didn't lie in the measurement part of their submission. He had not been lying when he'd said he was seven inches—and the photo showed that to be a solid seven, too.

Ding ding ding! We had a winner!

Something hit me hard in the back of the head. I screamed, jumping and almost sending my laptop flying to the floor.

"What the hell?" I snapped, tearing off my headphones and glaring at my brother. "Where did you come from and why did you hit me?"

Dom stared at me. "You're working? Here?"

Quickly, I saved the profile as The One and closed down my screen. "Well, yeah. Mimi knows. She doesn't care."

"I don't want another man's penis to be the first thing I see when I get here!"

"So? Look down your pants when you walk through the door. Oh, that's right. You still wouldn't see anything."

He flipped me the bird as Mimi walked in, wiping her hands on the bright-yellow, floral apron tied around her waist.

"Dominic!"

He threw his arms out. "I can't make a gesture at her, but she can look at male genitalia in your living room?"

Mimi crossed her arms over her plump body and stared him down with a fierce, dark gaze. "Dominic Austin, I remember catchin' you looking at female genitalia in my livin' room once upon a time, and that was for nothin' more than your own pleasure."

My older brother looked at me and her. "Mimi, she's looking at dicks for pleasure."

"Actually," I said, standing up. "I take no pleasure from looking at penises when they're being matched to someone else. Unlike you and your teenage porn obsession."

"Oh, yeah," he continued, following me into the kitchen. "Because you don't watch porn."

I pulled a bottle of water from the fridge.

Sometimes, it sucked that Mimi didn't allow alcohol in the house.

"I never said I didn't. That's the difference between me and you, bro. I don't lie."

"Lord, give me strength," Mimi muttered, shuffling over to the stove and continuing to pray under her breath.

"Are you calling me a liar?"

"Have you or have you not had a crush on Chloe since twelfth grade?"

Dom froze, blinking his long, dark eyelashes at me. "We're not talking about me, Peyt. We're talking about your penis obsession."

"As mighty convenient as that is," Mimi drawled, her no-nonsense attitude mixing with her deep Southern accent to cut through our immature sibling squabbling, "Y'all's dinner is almost ready, so set the darn table before I add human meat to this stew."

Both of us did as we were told. Dom grabbed all the placemats while I opened the cutlery drawer. It was the way we'd always done it, and it would never matter to Mimi if we were ten or twenty-something. Hell, even if we were fifty, she'd expect us to do it.

That was the rules. If we come for dinner, we set the table, and we clean up everything after.

I laid out napkins as Dom put three glasses upside down and got the water jug from the cupboard. By the time we were done, Mimi had a massive bowl of stew ready for him to set in the center of the table.

He grabbed it, and I picked up the plate of freshly baked bread to go with it.

My nose twitched at the delightful smell, and even my stomach rumbled, but I knew better than to touch that food until one: Mimi had her plate, and two: she'd thanked God for the food and prayed for our souls.

And everyone wondered where I got my dramatic streak from.

Mimi took a seat and held out her hands. We placed ours in hers, and she said, "Dear Lord, thank you for the food upon this table, and thank you for the strength to deal with my hellion grandchildren. And thank you for the strength to get through this dinner without beatin' them both with my spoon. Amen."

See? Dramatic.

If anyone needed beating with a spoon, it was Dom for starting it.

"Amen," we muttered, echoing her.

Mimi chuckled, pulled her hands from ours, and looked pointedly at Dom. "Well? You gonna serve your dear old Mimi?"

I bit the inside of my cheek.

"Mimi…" he groaned.

"I will make a gentleman outta you, boy."

"What about making a lady out of Peyton?"

"Hey!" I interjected, turning over Mimi's glass and grabbing the jug. "I'm a lady. I let men hold open doors for me, and I've never flashed anyone getting out of a car."

Dom stared at me. "Peyt, you once told me you'd only let a man hold a door open for you if he'd smack your ass as you walked past."

"Damn straight," I said, making sure Mimi had enough ice. "If he's holding the door, he better smack my ass as I pass. If not, I'll get the damn thing myself."

Mimi held up a hand. "Once heathen of a grandchild at a time, Dominic. You might need less work than her."

I opened my mouth, then shut it. I knew better than to argue with her.

"While I agree on that point," he said, shooting me a quick look. "I don't understand the purpose of serving you food. If I tried to serve a woman food on a date, I'd be up for getting castrated. Give her too much; she thinks she's too skinny. Give her too little; she thinks she's fat."

"Yeah," I said. "And if he pisses her off, he can't get laid."

"Young lady, you will watch that mouth at this dinner table, or I'll bend you over that sink." Mimi didn't even look at me, but I got the message.

Shut. The. Fuck. Up. Peyton.

I obliged.

Mimi then shot Dominic a similar look, and he quickly spooned some stew into her bowl. When he was done, he filled his own before leaving the spoon for me.

"And that's why you're no gentleman," Mimi said, tearing a piece of bread in two.

"She doesn't count," Dominic replied.

"Boy, 'course she counts. If you can't respect your sister, you think any self-respecting young woman is gonna take two looks at you past your pretty face? Psht."

I said nothing. I knew she'd have a smartass comment for me, too.

Really, it was a rookie mistake. He knew better than to play with Mimi.

If there was ever a woman who could mix modern with traditional, it was her.

Case in point: I could look at penis pictures in the living room but say "pissed off" at the table was worthy of a threat for a mouthful of soap. And there was no doubt she'd do it.

She'd probably break into your house and do it while you slept. Put it in your coffee. Mix it into your dinner. As long as you learned your lesson, she didn't care how it happened.

Nobody said another word while we ate, especially not Dom. Judging by the little sulk he had going on, he'd had enough of Mimi shutting him up tonight.

Which was, naturally, utterly amusing to me.

When we were done eating, Mimi excused herself to have a cigarette in the yard—which was how God gave her strength if you asked her—we got to clearing the table and washing the dishes.

"Heads, I wash. Tails, you wash." Dom produced a quarter from his wallet.

I sighed and leaned against the side. "Fine."

He flipped the coin onto the side.

Heads.

"Well, just as well. It's the most head you're gonna get," I said, turning off the tap and grabbing a towel to dry the dishes.

He rolled his eyes and pulled up his sleeves. "Now, I remember why I hate dinner with you."

"You've put up with it for twenty-seven years."

"And I should have killed you when I had the chance."

I glared at him and took the first clean plate. "I still have a chance to do it to you."

"Only if all the cocks you look at don't burn out your eyeballs."

"Dom, seriously! Unless you watch exclusive girl-on-girl porn, you willingly look at other men's cocks, too."

He froze. "And that's me switching to girl-on-girl."

"Look, bro, there's nothing wrong with looking at dicks."

"You would say that. Looking at them pays your rent. Shit, Peyt, you probably look at more cocks in a day than I look at my own."

"Yes," I said slowly, "But you have to find yours first."

"You're a bitch."

"I know." I grinned and put the stack of now-clean plates on the table.

He shook his head and scrubbed the side of a bowl. "Can I ask you a question? A serious one?"

"Uh...Sure. Go ahead."

Dom got the last bit of stew off the side of a bowl and put it on the side for me. "Do you ever get bored of what you do? Just making people hook-up?"

"No," I answered honestly. "Do you ever get bored of setting up relationships?"

"No, but I don't spend several hours of my working day looking at genitals."

"You just do that in your spare time, right?" I paused. "Right, serious. Put away the annoying little sister act."

He nodded.

"No. I don't. I guess... I get why people want a no-strings hook-up or even a series of them. Like the girl I was looking for earlier? She has a really great job, and she's super successful, and all the men she's tried to date are intimidated by her. But, she's also lonely. So, she wants someone she can meet up with a couple times a week, get dinner, and screw."

"There are people you can pay for that?"

"Ah. Why pay when I can find it for free?"

Even he couldn't respond to that.

"People really do that? Find fuck buddies through PAD?"

PAD. Because you didn't always want to say Pick-A-Dick in public. "Yeah. Some are accidental. They have great chemistry and keep seeing each other. Some people like my client from earlier is out to get a long-term, physical relationship without the emotional strings. The guy I think fits her wants the same thing because he just broke up with his girlfriend of three years. It works for everyone."

"Really?" Dom put the pot Mimi used to cook the stew on the side and looked at me. "Do you really believe people can have sex regularly and not feel anything for each other?"

I reached for the bowl, then paused. "It's just sex, Dom. It doesn't always have to come with an emotional attachment. You're not emotionally attached to someone you pick up in a bar and bone on the sofa, are you?"

"That's different."

"No, it's not. All I'm doing is scheduling a one-night stand with someone they're sexually compatible with. Why go out and risk finding Mr. Tap, Tap, Squirt, when I can find Mr. All Night Long?"

"Your mind is a warped place, little sister."

"What? Because I believe it's possible to have a sexual relationship with someone and not fall in love with them?"

He dropped the cloth in the sink and looked at me. "What? So you don't talk? Don't ask how anyone's day was? You just walk in and have sex?"

In an ideal world. "It's called friends with benefits."

"Friends with benefits don't work."

"Have you ever tried it?"

"Well, no, but..."

"Exactly?"

"Have you, Peyton?"

Aw, shit. "I have friends. Who I have benefits with," I answered lamely.

Dom folded his arms across his chest. "Have you ever had a purely sexual relationship with someone?"

"Fine. No." I threw my towel into the cooking pot. "I have people I've had sex with a few times, but not frequent enough to constitute any kind of a relationship with. But I know you can do it. Which makes me right, and you wrong."

His eyes glittered. "Prove it."

I stopped. "Wait, what?"

"Prove me wrong. Find someone in that little hook-up database of yours who you're "sexually compatible" with and prove me wrong."

"That's ridiculous!"

"No, it's not. You say it's possible; I say it's not. Someone has to test it out, and since I'm the one who has to be proved wrong, you have to be the test subject."

Well. The orgasms would be worth it... So would the satisfaction of proving him wrong.

I picked the towel back up. "What's the deal?"

"You sleep with one person three times in less than two weeks. If you can prove you're not in love with them, I'll give you five hundred bucks." He smirked. "If I'm right, you owe me five hundred bucks."

"This is getting more ridiculous by the second!"

"And I get to pick your hook-up."

"That's so wrong on so many levels!"

He held out his hands. "Well? It's down to you, Peyt."

"Let me get this straight. You want to go into my *confidential* database, pick a guy for me to sleep with three times, and not fall in love with, just so you can pay me five hundred dollars?"

"No. I want to go into your confidential database and pick a guy you'll sleep with three times, then fall in love with, so I get five hundred bucks off you."

"And this is why the Lord needs to give me strength," Mimi said from the doorway. We both jerked around to look at her, only to see her light another cigarette and turn, slamming the glass-screened door behind her.

Hell, she wasn't the only one he needed to give strength to.

CHAPTER TWO

PEYTON

Whoever replies 'K' to a text message should be chased into the ocean by pigs.

ME: I NEED A DOUBLE-SHOT HURRICANE WITH THAT PASTA.

Mellie: Peyton. It's midday.

Me: I am in CRISIS OVER HERE

Mellie: Chloe. Help.

Mellie: Chloe.

Mellie: Chloe.

Mellie: Chloe.

Mellie: Chloe!!! DON'T LEAVE ME ALONE WITH HER

Me: I AM HAVING A BREAKDOWN AND YOU'RE WORRIED ABOUT YOU?

Chloe: K

K?

K?

Fucking K?

Ugh. I wanted to stab something.

I hated that response with a passion.

I finished my coffee and set the mug on my desk. Running my fingers through my hair, I sniffed a few of the strands in the hope the sweet, coconut scent of my shampoo from this morning's shower would calm me down.

I'd hoped my conversation with my brother had been a dream. Unfortunately, the text I woke up to this morning proved that it wasn't.

He'd really challenged me to sleep with someone three times in two weeks and not fall in love.

It was stupid. So, so stupid. Why had I even entertained the idea? What the hell was wrong with me?

I didn't need to do this. I was happy with my sex life. I had my friends, and it was all fine. Why did I feel the incorrigible need to prove him wrong?

Aside from the five hundred bucks, it was because it was ingrained in me.

I was competitive. I needed to be the best. I needed to be right. I had to win.

I was a modern-day Monica Geller.

Which was why I'd enlisted the help of the girls. Screw Chloe's undying love for him, she knew I was right. And Mellie, well, she knew it, too.

I was right.

It was possible.

One. Hundred. Percent.

But why did I have to prove him wrong? Why couldn't he be the one to prove you could fall in love with someone in three hook-ups?

He was the one who needed to get laid, not me.

The front door opened, and Mellie walked in with Jake on her heels.

Great. Now the boyfriend was coming to girly chats.

"Oh, good, you brought back-up."

Jake grinned at me. "A pleasure as always, Peyton."

I poked my tongue out at him.

Mellie ignored our stupid exchange and threw herself down on my bright purple sofa, dropping her purse on the floor next to her feet. "All right. What's the crisis?"

I took a deep breath and let it out through my nose. I probably looked like an angry horse. "My brother—"

"Oh, shit," she muttered.

"—is an asshole."

"Yes," Mellie said slowly. "I became aware of that when he wedgie'd me in sixth grade as a dare."

I'd forgotten about that.

"We had dinner at Mimi's last night. He went on his usual shit trip about my job and how terrible I am and blah, blah, blah."

Jake's eyebrows shot up.

"Then, he decided to challenge me to prove that you can have sex with someone three times and not fall in love with them." I paced up and down the rug. "I mean, how stupid is that? What a ridiculous thing to make me prove. Of course, you can have sex with someone three times and not fall in love."

"Know that, do you?" Jake asked me.

I stopped and pointed my finger at him with a dark look before resuming my pointless pacing.

At least I was getting Fitbit steps.

Or I would have been if I was wearing it.

Come to think of it, where was it?

"This is bullshit." Pace. Pace. Pace.

"The fact I'm here and not having a nice lunch with my girlfriend? I agree," Jake said, leaning back on the sofa.

I hit him with another glare, and Mellie knocked her foot into his in a warning.

She leaned forward and looked at me. "Peyt, you walked into the challenge. You know Dom's the romantic of the two of you."

"That's not the point. The point is that my brother challenged me to be the one to prove him wrong. Why can't he do it himself?" Why was pacing so therapeutic? Or was that the ranting? "It's his stupid argument, not mine. I already know you can screw a person three times and not fall in love. I don't want to sleep with someone three times!"

"Is once your limit?" Jake asked, grinning again.

I'd had enough of him.

I jabbed my finger through the air at Mellie. "Control your human."

Mellie touched Jake's thigh and leaned into him. She lowered her voice and said, "Why don't you grab lunch and take it back to the office? Chloe will be back in a couple minutes. No offense, but you being here isn't helping."

No shit. All it was doing was winding me up even more.

Thankfully, he replied with, "Okay. 'Cause if I stay here any longer, I'm gonna climb onto the roof and take the outdoor elevator down to the sidewalk."

He leaned in to kiss her, and I mimed vomiting. He kissed her again before glancing at me and almost-waving on his way out. The sound of the door clicking behind him was music to my ears.

Don't get me wrong, I liked him, and he was perfect for Mellie, but we didn't exactly get along all the time. Mostly when I was in this kind of mood.

Then again, I didn't get along with many people anyway.

I finally slowed to a stop and looked at Mel. "What am I going to do?"

"Tell Dom no," she said simply, tucking her hair behind her ear. "You don't have to prove anything, Peyt."

"Tell him no?" Was she suggesting I lose? "Let him win? Hell no!"

The door swung open, revealing Chloe balancing two paper bags and two drinks holders. "Sorry, sorry! The traffic was awful. Here's your...double shot hurricane you asked for."

I almost snatched the cocktail from her and sipped. I gave her a grateful smile as she set down the bags and sat next to Mellie.

"Dom filled me in," Chloe said. "I told him he was fucking dumb. We all know you can screw someone three times and not fall in love. I told him to stop sharing your mom's Netflix account and watching her stupid emotional movies."

"Thank you!" I flung my arm in the air in a self-righteous swing of triumph. "And he'll pick the guy I get to screw based on who's in my database? That's bullshit!"

Chloe grimaced.

"It actually is." Mellie briefly met my gaze before she turned to Chloe. "I mean, he's the dater. He literally creates relationships. He's not going to pick the guy she can screw, he's going to pick the guy he thinks is most compatible with her."

"I know that," Chloe replied. "He'll probably pull someone from our database over just to screw with her."

"Noooooo!" I clutched hold of my drink and sunk down into the armchair next to them. I hadn't thought of that. Why hadn't I thought of that?

"Why don't we do it?" Chloe sat up. "I mean, think about it, Peyt. We're on your side. We agree with you. We'll pick a guy we know you'll never fall for, and Dom can't argue because we're impartial. We're not involved in this stupid bet."

Actually, that wasn't a bad idea. They'd pick someone I'd never fall in love with, or even consider falling in love with. They knew me better than anyone. This was totally doable with them on my side, right?

"Yeah, well, you better make me win. I don't want to lose five hundred bucks to that idiot." I sniffed.

"You bet five hundred bucks?" Mellie could barely get the words out through her shock. "Why?"

"Because! I need to be right, and if I win, he'll go away."

Chloe and Mellie shared a look. "Sure," Chloe said slowly. "Come on, Peyt. You don't have to prove him wrong, and you get to win. Let us do it for you."

"You know we're right," Mellie added, now scarily cheery.

Was I really going to do this?

Oh my God, I was. Because proving my brother wrong may as well have been in my DNA at this point in my life, and it would undoubtedly still be the case in thirty years.

I sighed and ran my hand over my face, then gave in. "You know what? Fine. What's the worst that could happen?"

***

"Okay!" Chloe sat down at my home desktop and opened up the website hosting site. She stretched her arms right out in front of her and cracked her knuckles. "How many submissions do you have in the "Unread" bit?"

I shrugged, curling into my armchair with a slice of pizza on a paper plate. "I don't know. Probably a hundred? The last couple matches have been easy to find."

"Okay. We're gonna use one of those."

"But, I—"

"Oh, good," Mellie said, coming in with three wine glasses balanced in her hands. She passed me one. "You told her, Chlo."

"Told me what?" I took the glass from her and sat up, almost knocking my pizza onto the floor.

They shared a look.

"What?"

"Uh…" Chloe slowly spun in my chair and looked at me. "You're not allowed to know who it is. We can't afford your endless vetoes just because you're picky as fuck."

"I have a right to have a say in who gets to go inside my vagina."

"And when you're on your date, you can happily refuse to have sex, and we'll come back to the drawing board," Mellie added unreasonably.

All right. Fine. It was entirely reasonable, but I felt unreasonable.

"You're taking this hell and turning it into a blind date?" See? I was so unreasonable.

Chloe grimaced. "Yes. Because you have to talk to the guy before you sleep with him, Peyt."

"I do?"

"Most people do that."

"I'm not most people."

"No shit," Mellie muttered, pulling my other armchair across the floor to the computer. "We promise we'll find you a pretty dick."

I snorted. "Right, and my vagina will smell like a freshly bloomed rose garden halfway through my period. Just find me a decent penis, okay?"

"That's more realistic," Chloe agreed, turning back to the computer.

I stared at them as I ate my pizza. I couldn't see the screen at all, and no lie, it was frustrating as hell. Mostly because I knew they were finding me someone to have sex with.

Hell, even I sent my clients a shortened profile and a facial photo before I set up meetings.

"What if they're not attractive? I need to see a photo first. I already had to pretend to be on my period once to get out of a hook-up. I don't wanna do it again." I was fishing now, and I knew it.

I could smell the desperation seeping out of my pores.

Ugh.

I hated not having control.

I put my plate on the floor and swung around in the chair, resting my legs over one arm and leaning against the other. I let out a low, long groan, tilting my head right back and cradling the glass against my legs.

"Oh, Jesus, here we go," Mellie muttered. "I don't know how you haven't got yourself an Oscar yet."

"Neither of you have nominated me."

"Hair color," Chloe demanded.

"What?"

"You can have a say. Think of it as guidelines. Also, I don't want to be the one getting poisoned because you don't like the date. So, give me a hair color before I change my mind."

Bingo.

"Brunette. No shade preference."

"Wasn't gonna ask." She wrote it down. "Eyes?"

"I don't care. I don't plan to look into 'em."

"Age?"

"Anywhere between twenty-five and thirty-two."

"Precise," Mellie noted.

I nodded in her direction. I knew what I liked. What could I say?

Chloe sighed. "Height? Body type?"

"Tall and fit. With just enough muscle so I can run my tongue down—"

"Cock size?" she blurted out, stopping me in my tracks.

I grinned. She was blushing furiously.

Mellie rolled her eyes. "Oh, Chlo. Why are you even asking this? The answer is long, thick, and hard."

"Like a math exam." I grinned even more.

"A math exam?" Chloe asked, looking back at me over her shoulder.

I sipped my wine. "C plus P equals O. Sometimes, O squared. Simple algebra."

"Do I want to know?"

Mellie put a hand either side of Chloe's head and turned her back to face the computer screen. "No."

"Never mind," she muttered. "I got it."

"Is that all the information you need?" I asked.

"It's more than I ever needed. Now, shut up and let me find you a fuck buddy before you make my ears bleed."

Never let it be said that Peyton Austin didn't listen.

I listened. I just tended to ignore a lot, too.

However, this time, my vagina's happiness was on the line. I'd listen all day long if it meant my friends could get it right—and help me prove Dom wrong.

Even if I was terrified.

And I was. I'd never actually hooked up with anyone from my website before. It'd all been through personal meetings. All me. No middleman—or woman.

What was I doing?

I'd gone and lost my dang mind. Mimi always said that'd happen.

I finished my wine and set the glass down on the floor.

God, what if they screwed this up? I wouldn't fall in love. Unless you were sweatpants or a brand-new donut place, I wouldn't fall in love with you.

It wasn't in my DNA. Some people could, but I wasn't one of them.

I loved. Don't get me wrong—I loved, and I loved passionately, but being in love was a whole other kettle of fish. One I didn't boil.

One I had no intention of boiling.

I leaned my head right back and closed my eyes, humming along to a tuneless song. I was totally making it up as I went along, but it was getting me through the hell that was this evening.

One day, I would be able to tell my brother to go screw himself, because these dares were stupid and immature.

Honestly, I'd hoped by now that would have happened.

"Done."

I jerked my head up. "What?"

"Done." Mellie grinned, leaning over the back of the chair to look at me. "We found him."

"You did? Oh, God."

"Don't worry. He's definitely not the kind of guy you could fall in love with." Chloe clicked off the screen and folded a Post-It note in half. "I'm going to contact him tomorrow."

"Who is it?"

"We're not telling you. You know that." She distorted her body on the chair and tucked the bright square into her pocket. "I promise he's hot, has a suitable penis, and you'll never fall in love with him."

I blinked at her.

That sounded like the punchline to a joke.

Oh, it was. The joke that was my life.

"I'm going to regret this, aren't I?" I groaned.

Mellie grimaced. "Peyt, you should have known that the second you agreed to do this shit."

Well, yeah, I knew that, too.

"We'll call you when we have the date set up." Chloe stood, picking up her phone. "And before you go searching, don't bother, Sherlock. I deleted your browser history, cookies, and everything except your saved passwords."

"And we deleted his profile." Mellie grinned, standing, too.

"I hate you both."

Chloe stopped in my office door. "And you should really delete your card info from your saved stuff. If someone hacks you…"

"They might put me out of my misery," I muttered. "You promise I'll win this stupid bet?"

In unison, they both crossed their finger over their heart in an 'x' motion.

Well.

That was fucking reassuring, wasn't it?

CHAPTER THREE

PEYTON

*Not all best friends are created equal. Unless they're mine.
Then they're both raging assholes.*

CHLOE: DON'T FORGET. 7PM. BILLIE'S.

Me: I'm half-dressed. I'm not going to forget.

I threw my phone down on the bed and leaned back against my bedroom windowsill. I lied. I wasn't even close to being half-dressed, but at least I'd showered.

That was how I stood now. Wrapped in my robe with my hair twisted up in a towel, staring at my still-blotchy-skinned reflection in the mirror above my bed.

I had no idea what to wear. Billie's was my favorite restaurant, and no doubt they'd picked that so I'd be somewhat comfortable in this dumbass situation.

But was there a dress code for this date? I'd worn both jeans and flats and dresses and heels to this restaurant.

Maybe the happy medium was jeans and heels.

Hmm.

I pushed off the windowsill and walked over to my dresser. My jeans were tightly packed into the third drawer, and I pulled out every single pair.

Aha.

There they were.

I pulled my favorite, light-blue pair from the pile and kicked the rest to the side, shutting the door. Flinging the pair onto the bed, I looked at the clothes on the floor.

Nope. Couldn't do it.

I crouched down, opened the drawer, and carefully folded every pair of jeans back up. I put them away, pair by pair, until they were ideally situated in the drawer, then closed it and went to the small bookshelf that housed my favorite heels.

Simple. If I did simple, I could go fancy on the shirt.

I pulled a Barbie-pink pair of heels from the shelf—my treasured Louboutins—and set them at the end of my bed.

Three t-shirt and eight underwear choices later, I had the perfect combination.

I put the underwear on, then did my make-up before letting my hair free of the towel. It was only just damp, and a glance at the clock told I had more than enough time to dry and loosely curl it.

Thank God for that.

***

I slid into the back of the taxi ten minutes before I was due to get to the restaurant. So, I'd be fashionably late. It being post-Mardi Gras only worked in my favor. Sure, there'd be the typical New Orleans traffic, but not enough that I'd be drastically, oh-shit-she-stood-me-up late.

Although, standing up wasn't a bad idea.

Shit, no, Peyton. We aren't doing this.

It was too late, anyway. I was in the back of this cab and on my way, and that was the end of that. I was going to see this date through, sex or no sex. Blind date or not, I wasn't going to have sex with someone I wasn't even remotely attracted to just to prove my brother wrong.

Aside from the satisfaction of being right yet again, I wanted a few orgasms out of this stupid little experiment.

The cab driver glanced at me in the mirror. "Blind date?" she asked, pushing a dark braid out of her eyes.

I nodded. "My best friends are assholes."

She laughed, pulling away as the light changed green. "Ain't everyone's?" She turned down the road to get as close to Billie's as she could and gave me the total.

I handed her the cash.

"Good luck," she said as she took it.

"Thanks. You keep the change." I smiled and, clutching my purse tightly to me, got out of her car. The humid air hit me immediately, and I blew a breath out as I walked onto the street.

The city was alive as usual. I sidestepped groping hands and overzealous drinkers with the expert skill of someone who lived here. Sure, it was early by the standards of most places, but it was practically twenty-four seven here.

I was sure that only Vegas or New York rivaled my city.

I stepped into the restaurant and sighed as the air con hit me.

The hostess greeted me with a grin. "A little birdie tells me you're here on a blind date."

I held up a finger. "Marie, don't you start. I'm stressed as it is."

She crossed something out on the paper in front of her. "Well, don't be. I saw him to y'all's table around twenty minutes ago." She rounded her station and leaned into me. "Girl, he is fine."

"So is my new rug," I drawled.

"No. I mean he's so hot I think the chef just served him up on a goddamn platter for you."

All right. Now we were talking.

"Then why are standing here?"

She snorted and touched my arm. "That's my girl. Come on. I messed around with the tables and gave you your favorite."

"You're a girl after my heart, Marie."

She threw a wink over her shoulder as we took to the stairs. I followed behind her as she dragged herself up them, three menus in hand. One drinks, two food.

Butterflies erupted in my tummy as we reached the small hall at the top of the stairs. I was mere feet from the person my friends wanted me to screw and not fall in love with. From the person who'd help me prove my brother wrong.

I was...

Excited.

And it was weird.

Marie pushed the door open. The sound of conversation bustling through the air hit me instantly, before I'd even looked up. The dim light of the upstairs seating area made it tough to see past the next tables and people and staff moving around, but the scent of the food hit me instantly.

"You're right there, Peyt." She pointed to the corner, moving off toward the guy with his head dipped, his face invisible to me.

I followed her through the restaurant. My fingers twitched against my purse straps, and my stomach was doing treble-flips with nerves.

I was not a blind date girl if it wasn't already +evident.

Please be perfect for this. I didn't want to do it all over again. My delicate sensibilities couldn't handle it.

I almost snorted at myself.

The only thing delicate about me was my panties.

"Here we go," Marie said, setting the menus on the plate. "Mr. Sloane, your date for the evening is here. Fashionably late, as always."

"Thanks so much." He looked up.

Our eyes met.

I drew in a sharp breath. Everything froze, and I swear to fucking God, my world stopped spinning on its goddamn axis.

No.

No.

They wouldn't have done this to me.

Time was a funny thing, wasn't it? The last time I saw the man in front of me, we were eighteen. It was our high school graduation. He'd held eye contact a fraction of a second too long, and in that fraction, I'd plotted his murder no less than seven times.

I couldn't be looking at Elliott Sloane, the one person who'd once broken my heart without ever knowing it.

No. There was no way. Chloe and Mellie knew what he'd done to me. There was no way they'd do this to me.

Yet, here I was, standing in front of him, on a blind date those bitches had set up for me.

I was going to kill them.

"No. Elliott?" I breathed.

"Shit. Peyton." His chair scratched against the floor as he stood up too quickly.

"What the…" I couldn't breathe. What the hell was happening?

Marie looked at us both and slowly set the menus on the table in front of us. "My name is Marie, and I'll be your server this evening. Let me know if you need anything."

With that, she turned.

I wanted to scream at her. Tell her there was no way he was my blind date. That she'd made a mistake. That she couldn't leave me here alone with him.

How could this be?

My heart was thundering. It was pounding so hard the echo of its beat in my ears was deafening, drowning out everything else.

What. The. Fuck?

Elliott looked around. "We should sit down."

I shook my head. "No. This is ridiculous."

He slid into his seat. "Then, by all means, be the center of attention. Nothing much has changed."

I wanted to snap his handsome little head off his neck.

I threw my purse onto the other chair and sat down opposite him. Without replying to him, I schooled my expression into one of extreme annoyance—eyebrows set, jaw tight, lips pursed—and threw my hand up for Marie's attention.

I wasn't going to give him the satisfaction of responding to him.

God, I hated him. I couldn't believe I was here. I couldn't believe he was here.

This was the boy who'd stood me up at junior prom. Who'd egged my car when I'd told him to go fuck himself when he asked me to senior homecoming, then who proceeded to shamelessly convince my date to ghost me.

He'd humiliated me.

And, because I'd mistakenly allowed my stupid little self to crush on him to the point of no return, he'd had a crush, too.

Except his crush had been my heart in the palm of his hand.

And now, I wanted to crush his neck between my own.

"Are y'all ready to order drinks?" Marie asked, doing her best to look disinterested in our situation.

"Wine. Large. Very large." I slammed the drinks menu down in front of her. I hadn't looked at it—I hadn't needed to. "We're done."

She hesitated, and that gave Elliott just enough time to order.

"I'll have a Coors. Thank you." He handed her his menu, shooting her a smile before looking at me. "You're ruder than I remember."

I stared at him.

I didn't want to talk to him. I wanted to punch him the face.

Hmm. Maybe getting alcohol wasn't the smartest idea, after all.

I folded my arms across my chest and stared at him. I had nothing to say to him.

Actually, that was a lie. I had plenty to say to Elliott Sloane, and every single thing started with, "Why?"

But nothing I wanted to say right now.

Right now, I wanted to ask him how he dared be so handsome. How he dared show up here with that perfectly coiffed brown hair. How he dared look at me with those captivating eyes the color of rich chocolate.

How he dared speak my name from between those full, pink lips. How he dared to be anywhere near me with all of that plus a stubbled jaw that was prime for stroking. Or those arms that, with one flex, could surely put a girl's eye out.

I wanted to ask him how he dared sit across this goddamn table and the first word out of his mouth be anything but a fucking apology.

But, I didn't. I swallowed the words. Ate them, along with my anger.

Well, most of it.

I let a little of it simmer below the surface. Let it slowly bubble away right down low.

Marie brought our drinks over and set them down on the table in front of us. "Are y'all ready to order?"

"No, thank you," Elliott answered. "Could we have another ten minutes?"

Marie looked at me. I shrugged a shoulder non-committally. I didn't care. I was stuck here anyway.

Walking out would only cause a scene, and despite my high school reputation for being a drama queen, that was the last thing I wanted.

"You got it." Marie tucked her pad back into her pocket and left us to it.

Elliott looked at me. "So, you're not going to say anything?"

"I don't have anything to say to you," I replied simply.

"Not even about how we ended up here?"

I curled my fingers around the stem of my wine glass. "For that," I said, lifting it, "You can thank Mellie Rogers and Chloe Collins."

His lips slowly curved up into an amused smile. "The Three Musketeers are still together?"

"Some loves last forever." I sipped my wine. "Mine for them has just run its course."

"I'm confused." Elliott sat back, tilting his head to the side. "Why is this their fault?"

I put the glass down and tugged at the collar of my blazer. "Between them and my brother, this is all their fault."

"You've lost me, Peyt."

"Peyton."

"What?"

"My name is Peyton," I said, looking him dead in the eye. "And you damn well know that."

I couldn't decide if the glint in his eye was amused or annoyed.

"You've lost me. Peyton." He almost added my name as an afterthought.

"Let's order food first. Apparently, I'm here for the evening." I caught Marie's eye and nodded for her to come over.

Elliott opened his menu and looked at it. "What's good here?"

"Everything." That was my standard answer. "Depends what you want."

"Y'all ready to order?" Marie asked.

I folded my menu and handed it to her. "I'll have the catfish po'boy, please."

"You got it, Peyt. And for you, sir?" She turned to Elliott.

"I'll have the same. Thanks." He passed her the menu, and when she'd gone, looked back at me. "Well? How is this date the fault of your sidekicks?"

I bristled, sitting upright. "They're not my sidekicks."

"Funny. Wasn't that always the case in high school?"

"You really don't want to flash back to sharing high school opinions." My voice held the edge of the taste of anger I'd kept hold of. "Mine won't be popular."

His eyebrows shot up. "You look older and you sound older, but you don't act like it."

I pushed my napkin away. "Screw this. I'm not doing this. I didn't want to be here in the first place. Sitting here opposite you just solidifies this as a giant crock of shit."

"Hey, hey!" Elliott held out his hands. "Sit down, Peyton. I'm sorry. I just…You make me feel like I'm eighteen again."

I hit him with a steady gaze. "Does that include being unable to hide a boner or make it last longer than thirty seconds?"

"Just the hiding thing. The boner has been there since I saw you walk in here."

If I were a blusher like Mellie, I'd be a goner.

Luckily for me, it took a lot more than cock talk to make me blush.

"And it can stay there," I said slowly. "Now, are you gonna put your inner asshole away long enough for me to tell you how we ended up on this godforsaken date?"

"When you put it like that…" He leaned back in his chair and looked at me, fingers clasped around the base of his beer bottle.

Great. This was going well.

I sighed and tucked my hair behind my ear. "Dominic decided to challenge me to find out if you could sleep with someone three times and not fall in love with them."

His eyebrows shot up. "And I'm assuming you're the test subject."

"At your service," I said dryly. "So, because I simply can't lose—"

"I'm shocked."

"—Here I am." I sat back, too. Did I?

Did I tell him I owned PAD? And that was how we got here?

Fuck it. I did. I was going to tell him.

"And you got roped into this, because, well." I twirled the stem of my glass between my finger and thumb. "I own Pick-A-Dick."

He choked on the mouthful of beer he'd just taken. The glass bottle made a thundering clunk as he slammed it down on the table so he could smack his chest.

Shit. That felt good.

I leaned back with a smug smile curling my lips. Surprise, asshole.

"You own the hook-up website?" he finally said after a moment of staring at me like I had two heads.

I nodded. "Dom and Chloe own the sister dating site. We all went into business together."

He raised his eyebrows. "Does that mean you saw my submission?"

A derogatory snort escaped me before I could stop it. "If I'd seen your submission, I'd have printed it off and burned it in my kitchen sink."

"Does that mean Chloe and Mellie saw it?"

"Oh, yeah. They saw it. And it'll be the last submission the bitches ever see," I muttered, bringing my wine glass to my mouth.

Elliott's eyes sparkled as he fought back a laugh. "I would agree, but how likely are they to help you win this dare?"

"I don't care. I'm about to find another person to carry out this absurdity with. I'd rather die than sleep with you."

"You wound me," he replied dryly. "Which is all the more reason to sleep with me."

"Because I hurt your feelings?"

"No, because you hate my guts, so there's zero chance of you ever falling in love with me. Hell, I'd die before I let you."

I paused. He did have a point. Having sex with somebody I already held a grudge against would work in my favor, especially if that somebody was Elliott Sloane.

Before I could answer, our food was brought over. After assuring Marie we didn't need anything, she left us to it.

I picked up a super-long fry and chewed down it.

Was I seriously considering this?

I glanced over at him. He was handsome. Devastatingly so, but then, he always had been. If his personality matched his looks...

Every female in the world would be fucked. Ovaries would explode from just being in his presence.

I was seriously considering this.

In a weird way, it made sense. I was attracted to him, and since I already hated him, there really was no chance I'd ever have feelings for him.

I clicked my tongue and reached for my wine. Elliott looked over at me as he bit into his sandwich. He definitely had a point...

Was I really going to do this? With him?

I was. Jesus, I was.

"Fine." I put my wine glass down and looked at him. "I'll bite my tongue and have no-strings sex with you three times to prove my brother wrong."

He held up his hands. "Whoa, I never said I'd do it."

I raised my eyebrows. "Really? You make a point, then try to tell me you aren't going to do this?"

"I said you had a reason to sleep with me. I never said I had one to sleep with you."

"I see you're just as much of an insufferable asshole as you were in high school."

"And you're as painfully frustrating as you were."

"I'm not going to offer it again. You're either in, or I'm leaving right now and going to shower six times to rinse the memory of the worst date ever from my mind."

Elliott sighed. "Well, who knows when the next time I'll be able to have a date will be? And I guess there are worse people I could have sex with than you."

"Wow. Talk dirty to me."

His lips tugged up. "There's only one condition," he said.

"I don't know if I want to hear this."

"I'm not going to ask to tie you up or do anything hugely kinky, Peyton. If I wanted kink, I'd tape your mouth shut."

I was regretting this already.

I glared at him and tapped my fingernails against the bottom of my wine glass impatiently.

He glanced at my rhythmic tapping before meeting my eyes. "We're going to your place. I don't want to explain to my babysitter why I'm bringing a random woman home."

I paused.

Babysitter?

"Your babysitter?" I blinked at him.

One of his eyebrows quirked up. "You don't know I have a daughter?"

"You have a daughter?" My own eyebrows disappeared into my hairline.

"I have a daughter," he confirmed. "She's three, and currently sleeping. And since my babysitter is my mom and they're at my house because my dad is sick, I'd really rather not take you there."

"How do you have a daughter?" I asked. I felt like my head was going to explode. "And why are you out with me when she's at your house?"

"Well," he started, "I have a daughter because I had this little thing called—"

"Don't be a dick."

He choked back a laugh. "She lives with me, full-time. I'm only here because my mother made me start dating, but I'd rather not date, and just hook-up. Even though the last time I did that I ended up with seven pounds of a tiny human to be responsible for."

I wanted to ask so many questions. Why she lived with him. Where her mom was. What their relationship was.

But, I didn't. Questions were bad, but this was good. He didn't want anything serious, I just needed to prove a point, and nothing really would ever happen, because not only was falling in love with him completely out of the question, I had no desire to be the person who took on someone else's child.

Or even my own. I'd leave that to my friends and be the cool aunt.

"Well, I can assure you I'm fully protected, and there's an unopened jumbo box of Trojan condoms in my nightstand. No tiny humans for me." I picked up my wine glass and looked at him. "Do we have a deal? We'll have sex three times in two weeks and never see each other again."

Elliott looked at me for a long moment. "Done."

CHAPTER FOUR

PEYTON

Multiple orgasms: the only thing which, in this day of social media, is designed to make men feel bad and inferior.

I THREW MY PURSE TO THE FLOOR AND SHRUGGED OFF MY jacket. "We need to set boundaries."

"We do?" Elliott asked, closing the door behind me.

"Yes." I hung my jacket on the hook and turned back to look at him with my hands on my hips. "Keep kissing on the mouth to a minimum. It's too intimate."

He nodded. "Agreed."

"Foreplay is necessary, but it doesn't have to result in an orgasm." I ignored the raise of his eyebrows. "This should be quick and rough. Got it?"

He held out his hands. "I can deal with that."

I headed for the stairs and started to walk up them. "When we're done, I'll disappear to shower. You should be gone when I get out."

"I have to admit, this is an efficient hook-up. I'm a little turned on by this."

I sighed. "Deal?"

"Deal. Trust me. I don't want to be here any longer than necessary."

"Thank God. It's so much easier if we're on the same page." I turned down the hall into my room. He was right behind me, and I knew I was crazy.

I was doing this. With him.

It was too late to turn back now. Besides—a part of me wanted to do this. He was ripped and toned with muscles that made my vagina want to weep with joy, and the way his forearms flexed whenever he'd gripped his drink at the restaurant had made my vagina weep with joy.

More to the point, the teenager inside me wanted to do this. She wanted to have sex with Elliott Sloane and prove to him what he'd lost when she, once upon a time, had liked him.

Petty as fuck, I know, but I couldn't help it.

Elliott pushed the door shut behind him and looked at me.

I hadn't anticipated this part. The going from the rule-setting to the actually-happening. Now, I was standing here in front of him, biting my lip, and looking him in the eye.

Tension made the hairs on my arms stand on end. I knew I needed to do something, so I reached down for my heel.

Instead, I scratched the side of my knee.

Elliott smirked, tugged his shirt from his waistband, and pulled it over his head. It fell to the side with a swish swoosh, gently landing on the floor with a sound that barely broke the silence between us.

I bent down and pulled off my heels, tossing them to the side. They hit with a clunk far heavier than the one his shirt had. He responded by undoing his belt and throwing it to the floor.

Goddamn it. Now, I had to take off my shirt.

I swallowed hard, bit the inside of my lower lip, and grabbed the hem of my shirt. Crossing my arms, I pulled it up over my head and tossed it to the floor on top of my shoes.

His gaze dropped, darkening as his lids lowered. His eyes swept over my upper body, from the hollows in my collarbones to the way the black lace of my bra curved over my breasts.

His Adam's apple bobbed. Desire darkened his gaze as he dropped it to the waistband of my jeans and back up again.

I was exposed. Totally exposed. It was as if he could see right through my clothing and see me naked.

He stepped toward me, and I tucked my fingers inside the belt loops of my jeans. I wasn't a nervous person—shyness wasn't a trait I'd ever been born with, so this was new.

Scary and new.

Elliott stopped merely a foot in front of me and looked at me. "Are you sure about this? Because I'm still wearing my shoes, and I'm okay with leaving with my shirt off."

I braced myself and met his gaze. "No, I'm not sure about this at all, but I'm going to do this anyway."

"Well, that's reassuring."

"Elliott?"

"Yeah?"

"Shut the fuck up and seduce me."

He didn't need to be told again. This time, he closed the distance between us completely. He grabbed my hip and tugged me toward him, then slid one hand around the back of my neck.

And kissed me.

Kissed me.

His lips touched mine, hard and firm. My heart jumped into my throat, and I inhaled sharply when his tongue flicked out across my lower lip.

His grip tightened, his fingers digging into my skin. Fizzes of heat tingled across my skin in lightning bolts, and my body melded against him as I felt the hot burst of lust through me.

Thankfully, he was fully in agreement with what I thought about kissing, and he quickly moved from my mouth to my neck. It was smooth, his lips ghosting across my skin in a swift movement. His fingers twined in my hair, and he pulled my head back so he could kiss his way down my neck.

His kisses were firm and hard, each one conveying the desire I felt currently pushing against my lower stomach.

My fingers found their way down to his pants and hooked through his belt loops, holding him against me. Despite my thoughts about kissing, I wanted him to kiss me properly.

It'd been so fleeting, yet it'd felt so good. How good would it be if he could do it properly?

I shook off that thought when he backed me up to the bed. He released his grip on me and pushed me back. I bounced when my ass hit the bed, but before I could ask him what he was doing, he pushed me onto my back and up the bed with a firm grip on my ass.

Elliott covered my body with his, sliding easily between my legs. His lips found mine again for a hot, rough kiss that made me arch my back and press my breasts against him.

His teeth grazed my bottom lip, tugging it firmly, and it was if that action set me on fire. My clit ached, especially when he reached between my breasts and unclipped my bra.

He pushed the cup away from my breasts and cupped it with his rough palm. It was just enough pressure that it felt good, but light enough that it didn't hurt.

Sensations flooded me as he dragged his mouth from mine and down to my chest. His touch was like lava against my skin—smooth and rich and burning.

Heat flushed across my skin with every movement he made. From the way his lips brushed my collarbone to the way his tongue circled my nipple.

Elliott moved further down my body, fingers probing and lips kissing as he went. He wasted no time sliding his hands from my waist to inside the waistband of my jeans.

He tugged. I lifted my hips so he could pull them over my ass and down and over my legs. I chewed the inside of my cheek as he removed them completely, leaving me in nothing but my pretty lace thong and matching bra straps.

His gaze roved over my body. It was dark and full of desire, burning with pure want, and I stared at his face. I wanted him to look me in the eye so I could feel the full effect of how he felt. I wanted to see him, raw and real, and I wanted to see every inch of him in this moment.

He looked up, and our eyes locked.

Dark and desperate. That was I saw when I gazed into his eyes. I wasn't entirely sure he didn't see the same looking into mine, but I was beyond caring.

All I wanted was for him to listen to what I'd said.

Hard and quick.

I'd meant it.

I wanted it.

I bit the corner of my lip.

I was tired of this playing around—I wasn't going to spend my night waiting for him to initiate foreplay. Fuck that shit.

I sat up and grabbed his jeans. Before he could say a word, I had the button popped open and his zipper down. My hands were slipping into his pants before he could even grab my wrists. By the time he had, I had the perfect view of his cock bursting out of his black boxer briefs.

I could see the head of his cock out of the top of the waistband. It glistened with pre-cum, and it was strangely satisfying to see he was as turned on as I was.

I leaned forward, pulling his cock from the material. Long, thick, and hard, I wrapped my fingers around the base and brought him to my mouth. Closing my lips around the head of his cock, I used my tongue to tease his very tip.

The dribble of pre-cum was thin and salty, and I used my saliva to make his whole cock wet.

I took him into my mouth properly, taking him further and further with each suck. He groaned, and his hips bucked more than once as he did everything he could to keep control of himself. His fingers stroked through my hair and fisted it at the base of my skull.

I looked up.

His head was bent, his eyes firmly on me as I teased him with my mouth. His neck was flushing red, and his eyes were dark and dangerously full of desire.

He pulled my head back, moving his hips, so I had no choice but to release him. He let go of my hair, and the next thing I knew, I was on my back, and he was bending down between my parted legs.

His mouth was hot as he kissed my legs and moved my thong to the side, so his warm breath was tickling across my aching clit. He used one finger to trail a path from my clit to my pussy, and he slipped that finger inside me easily.

His eyes met mine. "So wet for someone you hate."

I swallowed. "My body isn't as smart as I am."

"I think your body is a genius," he replied, keeping his eyes on me as he lowered his mouth to my pussy.

His tongue was like magic. He knew how to use it, and hot flushes ran through my skin as he fucked me with his fingers and toyed with my clit with his mouth. It felt so good—too good, and the way the pleasure was building inside me was so intense I didn't know much longer I could stand it for.

I tried to move away, but he wouldn't let me. He removed his fingers from me and grabbed my thighs. I was both annoyed and happy—annoyed because all this time was unnecessary, but happy because I was on the brink and desperately needed to come.

I did. Right into his mouth.

I was hot and sweaty, a total mess. He got up, wiping his mouth with a smug grin. He took hold of the waistband of my underwear and finally removed it, tossing it aside without a care.

"Condom?" he said, stepping out of his boxers.

"Top one." I pointed shakily toward the nightstand.

Jesus fuck, Elliott Sloane could lick pussy.

He opened the drawer and pulled out the condom box. It was brand new, bought especially for this purpose. I watched him as he pulled out one of the condoms and undid the foil packet.

Watching him roll it over his cock was mesmerizing. The smooth way his fingers made it fit to perfection had me squirming and trying to close my legs.

He smirked. "Flip over. Onto your knees."

There was a God.

I didn't need to be told twice. I flipped onto my stomach, then went up onto my knees. Elliott nudged me along the bed a little, and I went, clenching at his already-tight grip on my ass.

He positioned himself in my wetness, and with one hand on my ass, slowly pushed inside me. I dropped my head, closing my eyes as he moved fully into me and groaned.

It felt so good. He felt so good.

I hated myself for liking it.

Elliott moved, thrusting in and out. He was gentle at first, but after a minute or so, each previously careful movement became a deep, rough thrust that sent pleasure hurtling through my veins.

He slid one hand up my back and grabbed my hair. I gasped, moaning, too, and he pulled my head back, so my back was arched. He went deeper, harder, faster. I moaned, conflicted between how much I hated him and how much I liked this.

The orgasm hit me hard. He released my hair right at that moment and gripped my hips. He fucked me through it, and before he'd slowed, another rolled through my body.

"Oh God," I moaned, over and over. I could barely breathe through the intense pleasure that had all my nerve endings on fire.

He gave one final thrust, stilling inside me. His groan of release danced across my skin, and he collapsed over me, barely holding his own weight.

We stayed like this for a minute, so we could catch our breath, then he moved. It almost ached as he pulled out of me, but I ignored that feeling and rolled over.

Neither of us said anything for a moment, but he did throw me my robe. I was glad to cover up, which was a ridiculous thought, given that I'd just orgasmed onto his tongue, but whatever.

I stood on shaky legs and looked at the door to my bathroom. It was directly opposite my room, and I could see Elliott's bare ass as he cleaned himself up.

He was still half hard when he came back into the room and grabbed his boxers. He looked at me as he cleaned himself up.

"What?" I asked.

"Nothing. Just wondering if you were going to finish that prayer you started a few minutes ago."

"I will," I said, walking past him. "I'll say amen when you shut the front door behind you."

He laughed. "Enjoy your shower, Peyton."

"I'll be washing you off me. It'll be the best shower I've ever taken."

I slammed the door on his deep, full laugh. Locked it, too. Not that I thought he might come in and perv at me, but because I felt better with it locked.

I started the water and, dumping my robe on the floor, jumped into the shower without checking the temperature. It was way too hot, so I squealed and stepped away from the flow until it regulated.

I kept half an ear out for the sound of Elliott leaving. I didn't hear it as I showered, but when I stepped out, wrapping both my hair and my body in a towel, it was deathly quiet. I hung the robe up on the hook behind the door and stepped out into the hall.

He wasn't in my room, and a quick check of my office proved he wasn't there, either. A quick trudge down the stairs showed my house empty of him.

A sigh of relief escaped me as I moved to the front door. It was locked, and my key was lying on the mat by my feet.

"Amen," I muttered, putting the key in the hole. I quickly retrieved my phone from my purse, then headed back upstairs. After drying off and braiding my hair, I put some pajamas on, then put all my dirty clothes in the laundry basket in the corner of my room.

I had one more thing to do before I'd allow myself to sleep.

I grabbed my phone and brought up the three-way text chat with Mellie and Chloe.

Me: You're so fucking dead.

CHAPTER FIVE

ELLIOTT

Turns out, having sex with the girl you crushed on in high school was better than you thought it would be when you were eighteen. Even if there's a chance she was plotting your murder after in the shower.

PEYTON AUSTIN.

I don't know who I was expecting on that blind date, but it wasn't her.

The scariest part was that she hadn't changed a bit. She was still the same, self-assured, sexy, sarcastic person she'd always been. She still had that same scathing look that, when shot your way, made you feel two feet tall.

It was a skill—one I'd only mastered since becoming a parent.

I moved a stuffed Cinderella from the middle of the kitchen floor and set it on the table, then leaned back against the counter and looked out of the window.

God. I'd only signed up for the stupid hook-up website because my mother wanted me to start dating. I didn't want to date. I had no time to date. My life consisted of screwing up pigtail braids and hand-washing Disney princess dresses because *God forbid* they make them machine washable.

See? No time to date. Those dresses were delicate. Way too delicate for my work-roughened hands to clean.

Was three-years-old too young to make her do her own laundry?

I wiped my hand over my face and watched as a bird perched on a branch of one of the bushes in the backyard.

Peyton Austin.

Man. Fucking hell.

I ran my hand through my hair. What was crazier? That she was back in my life or that I'd agreed to her stupid situation? That I'd sat across from her and agreed to fuck her so she could prove what she wanted to?

She'd win that bet. There was no doubt about it. She'd been the bane of my existence in high school, thanks to the night of junior prom.

Hell, I remembered that like it was yesterday. It hadn't mattered that she'd been out of my league—at least, that was how it'd felt—or that I'd had other girls demanding my attention. I'd wanted her, and I'd damn well nearly had her.

Until my grandmother died, and I was dragged out of state without a chance to contact her to tell her. From that moment on, she hated me.

She wouldn't talk to me. She tore up the note I tried to pass her in math class, she ignored me in the halls, and she refused to answer my calls. Even when I finally was able to get the truth to her, there was no doubt she thought it was an excuse.

She was stubborn. Pig-headed. Obstinate.

Everything I hated, despite having my own healthy stubborn streak.

She held a grudge like nobody I'd ever known, and it was obvious that she still held it against me.

So, why did a part of me want to sit her down and convince her that the reason I stood her up was wasn't my fault? That I'd never meant to do it?

That, even at seventeen, she was the last damn person I'd have wanted to stand up.

I rubbed my hands down my faces. I hadn't lied to her when I said she made me feel like I was eighteen again. She was nothing but a pain in my ass. If I were a smarter man, I'd have walked out of there the second our eyes met.

Unfortunately for me, hours of Nick Jr. on the television every week had rotted a good part of my brain that controlled my common sense.

What the hell had I agreed to? There was something wrong with me. It didn't matter that she was as much of a spitfire between the sheets as she was out of them, or that one of the most surreal moments of my life had been her taking my cock in her mouth while she met my eyes.

Peyton was unlike anyone else I knew. She always had been. She was open and free and didn't give a fuck what I or anybody else thought about her. For all her bad qualities, this was one of her best.

Even if it meant we were both in trouble. Neither of us really wanted to be in this situation. The last thing I wanted was a Peyton-shaped blast from my past in my life.

I didn't want her obstinate, self-righteous, tight little ass in my life, even if it were only on the peripheral. I didn't want her mouthy, over-confident, drop-dead-gorgeous self anywhere close to me or my daughter.

Was that why I was standing here, half-dressed with a stone-cold cup of coffee to my right, thinking about her over and over?

I pushed off the counter and walked to the fridge and opened it.

"Ah! Daddy!"

"Crap!" I swung the door shut and looked down at my sleepy-eyed blondie. "I'm sorry, Bri. I didn't hear you coming. Did I hurt you?"

She rubbed her eye and shook her head, staring at me with her other eye. "No. But you saided a bad word, so dat means I get chocwat."

Damn it.

"It's a little early for that, don't you think?"

She shook her head in earnest.

"Well, I think it is. I owe you one with your lunch, okay?"

She sighed. "Fined. Can I had some breakfast?"

"You can. What do you want?" I bent down and pushed her light bangs from her bright blue eyes.

Briony pursed her lips and made a "hmmm" sound. I knew what she'd pick, and she knew it, too. It was the same thing every morning, but I still gave her the option to change her mind.

One day, I'd make her breakfast without asking, and she'd change her mind.

"Chocwat toast and a nana, pwease, Daddy," she said sweetly, smiling at me.

"Okay. You go sit at the table, and I'll bring it in for you in a second, okay?"

She nodded. "Can I used your tabwet?"

"As long as you click on the folder with your name," I agreed. "And don't turn the volume right up."

Another nod and she trotted off, pausing only to snatch the stuffed Cinderella from the table. She held both her and the stuffed Moana by the feet as she went.

I swallowed back a laugh and put bread in the toaster. I unpeeled a banana as the bread toasted and cut it up into a small, plastic bowl.

For the first time since I'd met Peyton's eyes, she wasn't the only thing on my mind. The mundane familiarity of making Briony's breakfast was comforting, and it pushed the brunette siren from the forefront of my mind to the back of it.

At least until I'd spread the Nutella on the toast, cut both slices into triangles, and delivered it and a cup of water to the living room. Briony was already happily playing her favorite game on my tablet, so after dropping a kiss on her forehead, I went to make another coffee and left her to it.

I rubbed my eyes as the machine sputtered out much-needed caffeine. What was I supposed to do now?

Could I really go through with this stupid three hook-up thing with Peyton? One down, two to go. But asking my mom to babysit two more times in the next two weeks... well, she'd get ideas. I'd already had a grilling from her when I'd gotten home last night.

I didn't need any more of those.

At the same time, I wasn't entirely averse to the idea. She'd made it perfectly clear that last night's dinner would be the only "date," something I was more than okay with. Talking to her wasn't exactly a completely enjoyable situation for me.

Not to mention she sounded like she wanted to bite off my balls every time she opened her mouth...

In hindsight... Letting her mouth near my balls wasn't the brightest idea. Maybe avoiding that was a good idea going forward.

I liked my balls in one piece more than I liked my cock in her mouth.

Maybe.

I sipped my coffee and stared at my phone as the screen lit up. A second later, it buzzed, bouncing lightly on the marble-effect countertop. Sighing, I picked it up and looked at the name.

My stomach dropped.

My lawyer.

I put down my phone and, with a deep breath, answered it. "Hi."

"Elliott?" he said. "It's Lawrence."

"I'd say it's a pleasure, but..."

"It's not," he confirmed. "She's going against the legal advice and is going to fight for custody of Briony."

I pinched the bridge of my nose. "Hold on." I pressed the speaker against my shoulder and stepped into the living room. "Bri? Daddy's on the phone. I'm going to be in the backyard, okay, princess?"

"Otay," she replied, her response muffled by food.

"Shout if you need me."

"Otay."

I took a deep breath and went through to the back porch. The wraparound porch was one of my favorite things about this house, but right now, it was only useful because the railings kept me on my feet when all I wanted to do was collapse.

"Sorry," I said. "I don't want her to hear it."

She was three. She wouldn't understand. But she still didn't need to hear this.

"Understandable," Lawrence said.

"How can she do it? Jenna gave up her parental rights. She signed them over one week after she left Briony at our front door."

"Grandparent rights are muddy waters," he replied. "There's nothing truly clear-cut about what they are and aren't entitled to. The letter from Bethany's lawyer states her daughter wasn't in her right mind when she signed Briony solely over to you, and that she's better being with what would be a two-parent family."

Anger bubbled inside me. "A two-parent family who haven't seen her since she was three weeks old. I offered. I told them I'd never keep her from them because even if her mother didn't care, I wouldn't take that out on them. They didn't care until two weeks ago."

Lawrence's heavy breath crackled the line. "I know that, Elliott, and so do you. We also know that she wouldn't benefit from living with them over you, but as I said, this is muddy waters. We offered them one weekend a month with her after you took sole custody, but I have a feeling this has been brewing since that day."

I clenched my jaw. "Well, now we pull that offer off the table. If they get her, they'll never give her back."

"Already reneged," he replied. "Now, I know you know this, but I have to advise you not to have any contact with Jenna's family or close friends at all, and I'd extend that advice to your family and anyone you may be close to right now. If they call, you don't answer. If they come to your house, you don't answer the door. Understand?"

"I understand," I gritted my teeth. "What happens now?"

"I'll respond to her lawyer and inform them of our stance. Unless Bethany and Vincent change their mind, we'll end up in a small court, at the very least."

Great.

"Great. Just what I need," I said.

Like I had the money for all these legal fees.

"The good news is that when they lose, we'll make sure they cover all necessary legal fees," Lawrence said as if he could read my mind. "We have both the moral and legal high ground, Elliott. Don't worry."

"Easy for you to say."

"Come into my office this week, and we'll talk about this more, all right? Let me do some research on similar cases. I'll email you when I have something."

Like I had a choice. "Fine. Works for me. Look—I gotta go. Bri is shouting for me," I finished on the lie.

"Sure. I'll be in contact soon."

I hung up and stared at the unlocked screen of my phone.

Three months. It'd be three months since I'd been advised by him that the parents of the woman who birthed my daughter were looking into gaining full custody.

We never thought it would happen. All we found told them no, it was a lost cause, you're wasting your time. We thought they'd listen—that we could arrange something amicably.

Three years.

It'd been over three years since her maternal family had seen her. Since Jenna had left her at my parents' door when I'd been at work. Since we got the note that she'd given up all rights to her.

Some people weren't cut out to be parents. She was one of them, and I'd had no idea until that day. I'd had no idea until I read the diary I had no idea she kept during her pregnancy. How she chronicled how she hated every second, how she resented my daughter, how she hated me for doing it to her.

How she'd have aborted her if she could have.

And her parents? Briony didn't know them. They hadn't seen her since she was small enough to be held lying in one of my arms. They hadn't cared to see her, although I'd lived in the same house for the past two years—a house they had the address of.

I locked my phone and shoved it into my pocket.

They could fight all they wanted.

There were few things in this life I really cared about, but I'd die before I'd lose my daughter.

And that was all there was to it. If they wanted a fight, I'd give them one.

CHAPTER SIX

PEYTON

Lingering feelings of hatred toward the guy you were with last night equals great sex, multiple orgasms, and a healthy dose of "What the fuck were you thinking?" the next morning.

WHAT THE FUCK WAS I THINKING?

Oh, that's right. I wasn't.

I hadn't actually thought about the fact I was going to have sex with Elliott Sloane. I hadn't thought about what it would feel like to kiss him or have his hands on my body. I hadn't stopped to consider what it would feel like to have my naked body under his, or his hands gripping my hips as he fucked me from behind.

I hadn't stopped to think for a second that he might be a fucking dirty talker.

Nope. It was classic Peyton. Do, don't think. Get on with it, don't consider it.

Now, now, now. That was me. Demanding and impatient and oh so fucking stupid.

I tore a big bite off my donut. A couple of sprinkles dropped onto my desk, so I licked my finger so they'd stick and tapped them all up to eat them.

Sugar. I needed sugar to process this.

I swear, I could still feel his fingers digging into my hips. If I touched my hips, they were still tender. He hadn't hurt me, not at all—and if he had, it'd felt too damn good then for me to register any kind of pain.

It was good. Great. Mind-blowing. Everything sex with Elliott Sloane had no place being.

I shivered, then took another bite of my donut to brush it off.

Goddamn him.

Goddamn me.

Goddamn my brother and my friends and this stupid thing called my life.

I hated Elliott. Hated him. With a passion. If you struck a match on my hatred, you'd have a nuclear explosion.

Was that why all I could think about was how hard he'd made me come?

Oh, I was so mad. I could feel it all snaking its way through my veins like a poison. I was so pissed at myself for having sex with him—I was even more annoyed that I'd enjoyed it. More than enjoyed it.

I licked frosting from my thumb.

I can't believe I had sex with Elliott Sloane.

Red-hot, filthy, dirty-talking sex.

And I'd liked it.

I'd liked it. I was attracted to him. Hated him, but attracted to him. Did that even make sense? I didn't know. Nothing much did make sense. Like how I'd even ended up sitting across from him in the first place.

Oooh.

My best friends were assholes.

Of all the submissions. Of all the guys. Of all the choices they could have made.

Of all the men on that website who were sexually compatible with me, they picked him.

My enemy. My arch-nemesis. The villain in my fairytale.

All right, I was exaggerating. He was nothing more than a decade-long grudge, and I sure as hell was not living a fairytale, therefore there was no room for a villain, but still.

How could they pick him? There had to be at least ten people on that site I could have screwed and happily got on with my life without.

I knew Elliott—or I had, once upon a time. But I still knew him. I remembered him. I remembered that he preferred baseball to football, he hated ice-cream, and he'd never seen an episode of Friends in his life.

Which was blasphemy, but I digress.

Or did he?

Did he still prefer baseball? Had he grown to like ice-cream? Had he finally watched an episode of my favorite TV show?

I didn't know Elliott. I knew high school Elliott, not adult Elliott. I knew the guy who snuck out after curfew, who played football because it made his grandpa happy, and who was a petulant jerk.

I didn't know the guy who'd sat across the table from me during dinner last night.

I didn't know the man who was a father.

And I hadn't allowed myself to ask. I was curious—too curious by nature, and that would be the one thing I'd have to curb if I was going to sleep with him again.

Questions. No questions. Not about him and not about his daughter. It was none of my business. The only thing that was my business was what was inside his pants.

I was only allowed to care about what was inside his pants.

And, you know what? The assholes who called themselves my best friends had been right.

His cock really was kinda pretty.

***

"I cannot believe you two!" I slammed Chloe's front door behind me.

A scream echoed. "Damn it, Peyton!" Mellie shouted when I walked into the open living area. "I almost cut my thumb!"

"I don't care!" I tossed my purse on the couch and pointed vigorously at them. "Y'all are lucky I don't cut you for the stunt you pulled!"

"I had nothing to do with it," Chloe said, cradling a wine glass.

"Lies!" Mellie pointed her knife at her. "It was your suggestion!"

I threw up my hands. "The betrayal! How could you do this to me? Why would you do this?"

"Settle down, Jennifer Lawrence." Chloe put down her wine glass. "The Oscars aren't evaluating this performance."

I glared at her.

"Okay, maybe in hindsight it wasn't the best idea."

"Maybe? Not the best idea? What part of you ever thought it was a good idea?" I was almost shrieking.

What? I'd kept this inside all day. The more I thought about it, the more their audacity pissed me off.

"You hate him," Mellie answered reasonably, tossing sliced sausage into the pan. "You've hated him for ten years. I couldn't think of a better person for you not to fall in love with if I'm honest."

"Did you even bother to read his profile? He has a child!"

Chloe poked her head out of the fridge and looked at me. "He has a child?"

Mellie turned. "He does?"

"Yes. A three-year-old daughter he has sole custody of. He was only on the website because his mom thinks he should start dating again."

"That's a lot of new information for someone you hate," Chloe pointed out.

"You sent me to dinner with him! Was I supposed to sit there and glare at him the whole time?" I mean, half the time was more than enough to convey my annoyance at the situation.

"You could have left." Mellie shrugged.

"And let Dom win? No way!"

"He didn't even know." Chloe shut the fridge, wine bottle in hand, and retrieved a glass from her cupboard. She poured.

"Keep goin'," I told her. "I want a real glass after the emotional distress you're putting me through."

Mellie burst out laughing. "Emotional distress? Oh my God, Peyt. You've lost your damn mind. If sitting opposite that hot piece of ass all night was distressing for you, then I think you've lost your touch."

"Hot piece of ass?" I questioned. "Hot piece of ass?"

"We saw his photos. All of his photos," Chloe reminded me as she slid me my glass across the kitchen island.

My full glass.

I sipped. "What do you want me to say? Yeah, he's hot. He always has been hot."

"He's hotter now," Chloe mused.

They were goading me. They weren't going to win.

"I can't believe you picked him. Just because I want to win doesn't mean I want to be tortured while I try to do it!" I huffed and leaned forward, resting my forearms on the countertop of the island. "Of all the people—"

"Here we go," Mellie muttered, throwing more sausage into the pan.

"I can't believe you'd pick him. You know how much he hurt me in high school. You know what he did to me and how he humiliated me."

"That was ten years ago!" Chloe said.

"Isn't that how long you've been in love with her brother?" Mellie asked.

"No!"

She was right. It wasn't. It was way longer than that.

"And we're not talking about me, we're talking about Peyton." Chloe turned to me. "Ten years ago. Can't you bury that hatchet to screw the guy three times? You're the one who agreed to Dom's stupid-ass challenge, Peyt. Nobody made you do it. By picking Elliott, we picked the guy we thought would help you win it."

"She's right," Mellie interjected, turning around. "We're on your team, Peyton. I guess we didn't realize you held such a huge grudge against him still."

"I don't still hold it," I argued. "It was brought back to life when I walked in there, and one look at him set my panties on fire."

"Whatever." She laughed.

"Look," Chloe said. "So he didn't work out. It's fine. We can find you someone else. Dom didn't know you had a date, so as far as he's concerned, we're all still looking for someone."

"Right," Mellie carried on. "And, he didn't stipulate when this stupid bet had to start by, so we have a ton of time. You went to meet Elliott, you sat through dinner, and you left. We were wrong."

"Ugh." Chloe dropped her head back. "I hate it when we're wrong. I so thought he'd be hot enough now that you could forget all that stuff and just sleep with him. Your vagina has more morals than I thought."

Oh, man, this was awkward.

"Well…" I paused.

They both jerked around. Chloe holding an onion as if she was going to throw it at me, and Mellie had the knife pointed right in the direction of my chest.

"This is not at all threatening," I drawled.

They dropped their...almost weapons.

"What was that "well?"" Chloe demanded.

"I know that "well." I've heard that "well."" Mellie turned off the stove and advanced toward me, Chloe on her heels. "Peyton, did you have sex with Elliott?"

"I, ah, um..." I pinched my finger and thumb together. "Little bit."

"Little bit? You can't have a little bit of sex with someone!" Chloe exclaimed. "Oh, my God!"

"I don't have to justify myself to you! I'm a grown woman! You're not my mom!" I ran backward and almost tripped over the coffee table as they wrestled me onto the sofa.

Chloe launched herself on top of me and stretched across the sofa so I couldn't move. "Tell us!"

"No!"

Mellie grabbed two books off the shelf next to the TV and brandished them at me. "Tell us the truth or the books get it."

My eyes widened.

"That's right," she continued, an evil glint in her eye. "You tell us the truth, or I'm putting these books back on the wrong shelves, and the sizes will be all mixed up!"

I whimpered.

She put the bigger book on the shelf with the smaller ones.

Oh, man.

"Hey," Chloe said. "Be gentle. The books aren't the ones being a dramatic, stubborn idiot."

"Fine!" I squirmed. "Put the books back. You know I hate it when you do that."

"Are you gonna tell us?" Mellie questioned.

"Yes."

"Say it," Chloe demanded. "Say the words right now."

I took a deep breath. "I had hot dirty sex with Elliott, and I liked it!"

I clapped my hands over my mouth.

They both gasped.

Mellie dumped the books on the table, and Chloe climbed up off me. I shook out my arms and legs and sat up properly.

"I had sex with him," I said again. "He wanted to know how the hell we ended up having dinner together, so I told him everything, and there you have it. He agreed to be the guy I sleep with since he agrees I'll never fall in love with him, and that's the end of it."

"So, you came in here screaming and shouting about us picking him, only to tell us that you had sex with him anyway?" Mellie asked.

I paused. "Pretty much."

"Hot, dirty sex that you liked?" Chloe continued.

"I don't have to justify myself to you. And for God's sake, let me put those books back!" I got up and grabbed the books from the table and put them back.

Thank God for that.

Nothing annoyed me more than mixed book sizes.

Or just disorganization in general.

"You hate him!" Mellie laughed. "Of course, you have to justify yourself. At the very least, you have to justify the bitch fit you just threw."

"You had no right to pick him."

"But you had a right to sleep with him?"

I held out my hands. "My vagina, my rules."

Chloe stared at me for a second before she burst out laughing. "Okay, first, Mellie? Your sausage is burning."

"Shit!"

"And, Peyton? Sit down, because we need to hear more about your—"

"Don't you dare finish that sentence."

***

Unknown: Your friends really suck at privacy.

I blinked at the message notification on my phone screen.

It was five-fifteen in the morning. Who was the sadist texting me this slightly ominous message?

I sat up in bed and flicked the switch for the lamp on my nightstand. The room flooded with a dim, warm light, and I pulled the covers up over my waist as I propped myself up on my elbow to reply.

Me: Who the fuck are you and why are you texting me at this sadistic hour?
Unknown: It's Elliott.

Of course, it was. I saved the number before I replied.

Me: How did you get my number?
Elliott: Chloe and Mellie are not good at protecting your privacy.
Me: Color me surprised. But that doesn't answer the question of why you're texting me at five in the morning.
Elliott: Couldn't sleep.
Me: And you didn't have anyone else to text?

Elliott: Not anyone I can text saying, "Hey, don't you need more sex to stay on track with your bet?"

Me: I feel like we're potentially entering into sexting, and I'm not sure how I feel about that.

Elliott: Does sexting count to your total?

Me: I'm gonna say no to be on the safe side.

Elliott: Damn it. In that case... Never mind.

Whoa, whoa, whoa.

Me: Never mind? Never mind what?

Me: You don't get to wake me up at five a.m. and leave me hanging.

Elliott: If I tell you, you might kill me.

Me: Got plenty of reasons left in the bank from high school to kill you, buddy.

Elliott: You interrupted my sleep, and now I have a raging hard-on because I woke up too early.

Oh.

Ohhhh.

I fidgeted in the bed, clamping my legs together. Why was the idea of him having a dirty dream about me kinda hot? And why did I like it?

Goddamn it. Where was teenage Peyton and why wasn't she reminding me of all the things I hate about him?

Me: That's hardly my fault. I didn't WANT to wander into your dreams.

Elliott: I thought I'd gotten rid of this problem after graduation.

Wait, what?

I sat upright, the covers now pooling around my stomach.

He dreamed about me in high school?

Me: You dreamed about me in high school?
Elliott: Me and half the other guys in our year.
Me: That's why I stayed a virgin until after graduation. I wasn't about to lose my virginity to some two-bit fuckboy who'd only ever made out with his right hand.
Elliott: And that's the most accurate description of our graduating class I've ever heard.
Me: Did it cure your boner?
Elliott: No.
Elliott: Honestly, I'm a little torn.
Me: On what?
Elliott: Half my high school fantasies about you in senior year were you on your knees, and since that actually happened…
Me: I hated you throughout the entirety of that year.
Elliott: I know. But horny teenage boy > pissy teenage girl.
Me: Watch it, or I'll come over there and slap your cock back to soft with a fly swatter.
Elliott: All I'm saying is that if you're not averse to lying on your side and being fucked from behind, it can be arranged.

Oh, God. There was another squirm.

Elliott: Really hoping you aren't against it, because I can't stop thinking about lifting up your leg and playing with your clit while I fuck you.

I swallowed and clamped my legs together. No. I was not going to get turned on by his messages. Not at this time of the morning. Not ever.

Even if now I was the one who had that image in my head. Me on my side, him behind me, my hand holding my leg up while his sneaks between my legs to play with my clit...My back arching while he—

Fuck it.

There it was. My clit ached as a gentle flush of heat ran through my veins. I was turned on, and now I was screwed. I wouldn't be able to get that idea out of my head. That picture would be with me until it happened.

Me: I'm not listening to this.
Elliott: You're wet, aren't you?

Yes.

Me: Even if I were, I wouldn't tell you.
Elliott: I'll see you later.

What?

Me: You will?

He didn't reply.
And I was wide awake.
Awesome.

CHAPTER SEVEN

PEYTON

Plot twist: masturbating to porn doesn't stop you wanting to screw the guy you hate. That's what they should have taught in sex ed classes.

HOT. BOTHERED. FRUSTRATED.

Those three words all accurately summed up how I felt when I walked into my office at nine a.m. I was tired, and not even watching porn had managed to get rid of that ache I'd felt ever since that text from Elliott.

And, I didn't care how desperate I was, I wasn't going to masturbate over him.

Hell, I didn't even want to text the guy.

Right now, I didn't even want to see him. Given the fact it'd only been two days since what I was now referring to as Hook-Up One, it was too soon. I had two weeks, not four days.

There was no rush for round two.

No matter how much my hormones disagreed.

I dumped my purse on the floor next to my chair and sat down at my desk. My head was thumping, so as I fired up my computer, I dug around in the drawer for some painkillers. Two Tylenol were languishing in the back of the drawer, still in their little plastic packaging.

Who knew how long they'd been there?

Did painkillers have an expiry date?

Was my headache so bad that I would risk it?

Hmm.

Not quite ready to risk my life for relief, I pushed the strip to the side and logged into my PC. I'd shamelessly ignored my emails for the last twenty-four hours while catching up on some matches, and now, I was paying for it.

I was not okay with eight hundred emails in a day and a half.

This was why I drank a lot.

I pulled a bottle of Coke from my purse and loaded my email. The number blinked at me annoyingly, and I

sighed before running my gaze over the never-ending
unread list.

Submission. Submission. Submission.

Oh, man. That was a lot of dick pics.

Thankfully, they were all in the online portal, and
these were just the notifications.

I made it through five pages of them before my
office door opened. There was no knock, which meant
it was one of two people: Chloe or Dom.

I hoped it was Chloe.

I looked up.

It wasn't.

My brother grinned. "Hey, shithead."

"What's up, asshole?" I asked, deleting another page
of notifications.

I really needed to switch that function off.

"Busy?" he asked, pulling the chair opposite my
desk out and sitting down. "Whatcha doin'?"

"Working." I glanced around the side of my
desktop. "Clearing out my emails."

"You really should turn off those email
notifications."

"Thanks for the idea, Einstein," I muttered, deleting
another page. "What do you want?"

Dom leaned back, linking his fingers behind his
head. "What? Can't a guy drop in on his favorite
sister?"

"First," I said, holding up a finger and finally giving
him my full attention, "It's not dropping in when your
office is the other half of this building, and your
apartment is right upstairs. Second, I'm your only sister,
so am, by default, the favorite. Sadly."

He waved his hand in dismissal. "All right, whatever. Chloe isn't here yet, and I lost my key to the office."

"You keep that on your house key."

He just stared at me.

"Boy, I do not know how Mom ever allowed you to move out."

"She got fed up with me losing her keys and decided I should lose my own instead."

Responsible parenting at its finest.

I opened the other top drawer and unzipped a small pouch. Removing the shiny, silver key, I closed the drawer with a flick of my elbow, then slid the key across the top of my desk.

"There," I said. "The spare. Bring it back as soon as you unlock your door."

"It's like you think I'll lose it." He grinned.

"I don't think you will; I know you will."

His grin only widened. "So. How's the experiment coming along? Chloe said they'd found you someone."

Clearly, I wasn't going to be able to work in the immediate future.

"Yep. We had dinner," I said evasively.

"Dinner? You had dinner?"

"What? You want me to sit here and detail every inch of the date with you?"

Dom dropped his hands and rested one arm on the arm of the chair. "Can I not ask?"

"About what? Him, the date, or the sex? 'Cause I'm not gonna lie, I'm not into discussing the sex with you."

"Him," he said.

Did I tell him? Was I able to tell him? Was there a rule that said his name had to be disclosed? Or that I couldn't know the guy before we had sex?

No. No, there was not.

I leaned back in my chair and folded my arms across my body. Then, I waited until my brother had shamelessly picked up my bottle of Coke and taken a mouthful before I said, "His name is Elliott Sloane."

He choked on my drink, slamming the bottle down on the desk.

Man, that was satisfying.

Dom thumped his fist against his chest, coughing out the last of his shock. "Isn't that the guy in your class who was quarterback?"

I hit him with a thunderous glance. "And the guy who stood me up junior prom."

"Ah, shit, yeah!" He snapped his fingers. "Didn't you blow him off after that, so he egged your car?"

I mumbled something into my hand.

"You did! Then, he told Todd Simpson not to go with you to homecoming because you were sick."

"I was not sick!" I gasped and slammed my hand on the desk. "Elliott was a dick, and you know it!"

"Says the person sleeping with him."

I held up one finger and leaned forward on the desk. "You never said he had to be a stranger. Chloe and Mellie picked him for me. I had no say in the matter."

"I knew they shouldn't have been given free reign on this. You already hate that guy—this is unfair."

"You didn't say it had to be a stranger." I reached for the bottle of Coke and quickly changed my mind.

I'd shared baths with my brother as a kid—I didn't want to share saliva as an adult.

"I dropped the ball there," he muttered, picking up the Coke bottle I'd just discarded.

I was glad he was enjoying it.

I wasn't. I wanted to punch him. The joys of siblings...

I held up my hands. "You never said, they took advantage, and I'm just here to prove you wrong. Don't take it out on me."

He made a non-committal grunting sound and took a long drink of *my* Coke. "I'm not happy about this."

I got up with a raise of my eyebrows and went to the window to open the blinds. "I'm not happy about this, either, and I'm the one who has to have sex with a guy I hate. Suck it up."

"Have you ever had sex with a guy you actually like?"

"Dom, I will come over there, and I will rip your head from your puny little—"

"Oh, give it a rest," Chloe said, standing in the doorway with her hands on her hips. "It's too early for y'all's fighting."

"She started it," Dom muttered.

I walked past him to my desk and smacked him on the back of the head. He winced but refused to acknowledge it otherwise.

"I don't care," Chloe said, putting her purse at her feet so she could shrug off her leather jacket. "I woke up late and didn't get coffee yet, so y'all quit your bitching before I make you."

Ah. She was lovely before caffeine. Definitely the girl you'd take home to meet your mom.

"Then get your coffee," Dom said to her, "Because we need to talk about that stunt you pulled."

She paused. "What stunt?"

I sat in my chair and spun side to side, grinning.

Recognition dawned on her, making her jaw drop. "Ohhhh," she said. "Elliott Sloane. Yeah, that was all Mellie."

"No, it wasn't." I grinned even more. "It was both of you. Equal parts responsible for it."

"I'm not—I didn't..." She grabbed her purse and looked between us. "I don't have to listen to this. I have work to do."

"So do I. I have a meeting in ten minutes, so get out of my office." I looked pointedly at my brother as I said that.

He held his hands up like leaving was a huge hardship and stood up. "You're in a shit mood today."

I stared at him. "You owe me a bottle of Coke."

He looked at the bottle that had been mine, then shrugged and grabbed it. "I still owe you a candy bar from when you were eight, and you haven't gotten that yet."

"Get out," I deadpanned. "Before I kill you."

"Lord, give me strength," Chloe breathed, shaking her head. She walked away from the office to hers across the hall. "Dom, have you even been in here yet?" she shouted.

"He lost his key again!" I yelled at her.

My brother raised a fist and shook it in the air. He looked torn between shouting at me or throwing something at me.

I was saved by my best friend walking back into my office.

"You lost it again?" she asked, staring at him. "I gave you two spares last time!"

Dom muttered something I couldn't understand.

"You lost them both?" Chloe was near hysteria now. "How? How are you allowed to live unsupervised? That's four keys in a year, Dominic!"

He opened and closed his mouth. Nothing came out.

You know when you were a kid, and your sibling got blamed for something you did? That sheer, smug delight that reached from the top of your head to the tip of your toes?

I felt like that watching this. Only this was better because Chloe was soft but fierce, and if you pissed her off, you knew about it.

The fact she was sans caffeine only made this more interesting.

"You know what? I'm not getting you another." She folded her arms across her chest. "Until you can prove you're not going to lose it, I'm not doing it."

"It's a business expense," came his response.

Idiot. He should have apologized and told her she looks pretty today.

"I don't care." She jabbed her finger at him. "You're dumb. You're almost thirty. Now, I have to call to get the locks changed because God only knows how many people have the key to our office where we keep confidential information on a good portion of this city's residents."

I needed popcorn.

"Good, then the locksmith can give me a key." Dom shrugged his shoulder.

"No. The only key you're getting is the WiFi password so you can learn how to be a responsible adult!" she snapped, right before she turned and stormed into her office across the hall.

Neither I or Dom said anything for a minute. Then, he turned to me. "At least she didn't throw anything at me this time."

There was that.

I met his eyes. "Seriously. Just sleep together already. I can't take it anymore."

He scoffed and wandered to the door. "Sure. You can't take it."

That was the closest admission I'd ever had that he wanted her. Maybe they needed a nudge.

Hmm…

"Don't." He stopped and pointed at me. "Don't, Peyton."

I held up my hands. "I'm not doing anything."

He stared at me for a good minute before he left, closing my door behind him.

I hoped he was going to Starbucks before he went into his own office. Otherwise, it was his funeral.

***

"Perfect," I said into the phone, writing down what the client on the other end of the line had just told me.

"When can I expect to hear from you?" the sweetly-spoken lady said.

"It will take me a couple of days to match you," I said. "So, expect the end of the weekend."

"That's perfect. How many options will I have?"

"Between three and five men depending on your compatibility."

There was a knock at my office door, so I got up to answer it, holding the phone to my ear still.

"Awesome, thank you. Do you need anything else from me?"

I opened the door and almost choked on my own saliva.

"Ms. Austin?" the woman on the phone said.

Dark hair. Dark eyes. Jaw that could cut glass. Complete with a dirty white t-shirt and ripped, paint-covered jeans, plus work boots.

I waved Elliott into the office. "Sorry—a bird flew into my window."

Elliott held his hand over his mouth to stifle his laugh.

"It would be helpful if you could send me some form of a schedule," I said, putting my head back in the game. "Availability is one of the things I have on the application form for the men, so knowing any times you're not free to meet or if you have any preferences will really help me narrow down the field from the get-go."

"I can send that over to you today. I'll have my assistant pull up my schedule for the next month. Thanks so much."

"You're welcome, Sandie. I'll look for your email."

"Perfect. Have a great day!"

And just like that, she hung up.

Elliott raised his eyebrows. "Client?"

I nodded. "Some high-flying businesswoman who wants to get laid without having to worry about whether or not her toilet seat is down how it should be. I feel that on so many levels."

He chuckled, taking the seat Dom had been in this morning. "That's why there are two toilets in my house. One is pink and has a fluffy rug, and a hand-drawn sign on the door that depicts me with a big red cross."

It was my turn to laugh. "I'm not much of a kid person, but I think I like yours already."

He smiled. His eyes lit up a little with pure love, and it was weird seeing that on him. "Briony's a spitfire, that's for sure. Which is why I plan to keep her away from you at all costs since she doesn't need help in the attitude department."

"If I even remotely cared what you thought of me, I'd probably be offended by that."

"You get offended?"

"Only when people tell me powered donuts are better than ones with sprinkles." I leaned back in my chair. "To what do I owe the displeasure of this visit?"

He clutched his chest over his heart. "You wound me, Peyton."

"Get on with it, or I really will wound you. I have emails coming out of my ass." Right on cue, my phone rang. "Hold on." I held up a finger and answered. "Good afternoon! You've reached Pick-A-Dick, Peyton speaking. How can I help you?"

Elliott buried his face in his hand, silently laughing.

I had to look away before I laughed, too.

My business name was ridiculous. I loved it.

"Hi. I was hoping I could make an appointment with you?" a shy voice said.

"Absolutely. When were you thinking?"

"Next week?"

"Give me a second." I flicked over the page of my planner. "I can do Tuesday at two-thirty. Does that work?"

"Yes. Thanks. My name is Rhianna."

I scribbled down her name—probably spelled wrong—and clicked my pen. "Perfect. I'll see you then."

"Great. Thanks. Bye." She hung up quickly.

I dropped the phone unceremoniously onto my desk.

"Who knew so many people needed to get laid?" Elliott quipped.

"You have no idea," I said, clicking off my email screen so that number wasn't terrorizing me anymore. "Or, maybe you do, since you signed up."

"It was a date or get laid. I only have time for one of them."

"Yet, here you are, in my office. Why aren't you working? Wait, where's your daughter?"

His eyebrows shot up. "I happen to be on a thing called a lunch break. Do you take those? And Briony is at daycare, talking their ears off instead of mine."

"Unless Chloe brings me food? No. Have you seen my emails today?" I waved a half-hearted hand at my computer. "I don't have time to eat."

"Aren't you hungry?"

"Sure, but that just means I get extra ice-cream after dinner." I shrugged. "I'm self-employed. I don't work, I don't make money."

"How do you make money at this?"

I twirled a lock of hair around my finger. "You didn't read the website very well, did you?"

"Desperate times," he said solemnly.

"You get two weeks free, then you have to pay me for the pleasure of being pleasured."

"Just the guys pay?"

"No, but given the trauma I sometimes experience thanks to dick pics, I probably don't charge enough."

"How much is it?"

"Twenty bucks a month."

"Twenty bucks a month?" Elliott's eyebrows shot up, but his lips curved into a small smile. "People seriously pay that?"

I held out my hands. "You say that like I'm charging people a mortgage! I have to look at dick pics. Matching them is a lot of work. I'm not matching on personality—I'm matching whether or not two people are going to walk into the bedroom and get their minds blown."

"Surely there's some level of a personality match."

"Obviously. I'm not going to match a BDSM-loving Dom with someone who doesn't know where the nearest sex shop is."

He stared at me for a second. "Where is the nearest sex shop?"

"Two blocks that way." I nodded to the left.

"Do you go there regularly?"

I pulled a card from the holder in front of me and tossed it across the desk to him. "Regular enough that I have my own discount count. Here. They do those vibrating vaginas for men. Now you don't need to date or get laid."

CHAPTER EIGHT

ELLIOTT

People will always surprise you. Like how a toddler can have a rotting banana skin in their room for a week and not care. Or how your high school fantasy hands out personal discount codes for vibrators.

"YOU HAVE A DISCOUNT CODE?" I PICKED UP THE CARD she'd thrown at me and flipped it over. Yep. There it was, big and bold on the back with the name and address of the adult store.

"Why wouldn't I? I send people their way all the time." She swung her heeled feet onto the desk, crossing them at the ankle, showing off her long, bare legs.

"Doesn't sending people to an adult store defy the object of you helping them to get laid?" I raised an eyebrow and put the card back in the holder.

I didn't need her discount code. For now, I had her.

"No. In fact, it works in my favor."

"How?"

She sighed as if she had better things to do, and she probably did. God only knew she'd mentioned her emails enough, but after spending half my night dreaming about fucking her senseless again, I wanted to see her.

"It doesn't matter how good the person you're sleeping with is if you don't know what you want. If you don't know how to make yourself come, you can't expect anyone else to." She said it so matter-of-fact, like it was obvious. "Sometimes, some of the women who come to me don't know their own bodies. I had a thirty-something-year-old woman come in after her divorce last year. She married her high-school sweetheart and had only ever slept with him. The sex was fine, but she wanted more, and she admitted that she didn't know how to pleasure herself. I gave her tips and sent her to the store. Two weeks later, she came back for her match, and now she comes in every few months for a new guy and raves about her mind-blowing sex life."

I stared at her. "All that from a couple of dildos?"

"There's more to female sex toys than dildos and vibrators. Bullets, eggs, balls—"

"Balls?" That sounded...peculiar.

"Balls," she confirmed. "They're metal weights on a string you put in your vagina and have to hold in place with Kegels. They rub against the g-spot."

"You sound familiar with them."

Unashamed and without batting an eyelid, she said, "You're not a plumber, so you wouldn't tell someone how to fix their leaky sink. You'd tell them how to build a wall. I can't tell my clients how they should look into learning about their bodies if I don't know about mine."

Hell, this woman was something else. She wasn't even blushing. She wasn't shy at all about what she was saying. It was black and white to her.

It didn't affect her, but it was sure as fuck affecting me. Now, all I could think about was how she'd look with those damn balls. How did she put them in? Did she play with herself to make herself wet first?

Did she blush when she walked with them in place?

I leaned forward to hide the fact my cock was rapidly hardening in my pants.

Not that it mattered. She didn't miss a damn thing.

Her lips twitched up the tiniest amount, but it was the knowing spark in her eye that told me she knew.

The biggest problem was that Peyton Austin was hot as fuck, and she knew it. She played on it. Her looks and her not-quite arrogant confidence made for a heady, sexy combination. She was self-assured. She knew what she had, and she used every little bit to her benefit.

"You are the most unashamedly honest woman I've ever met," I admitted. "And if I hadn't already fucked you blind, that might intimidate me a little bit."

"How is that even remotely intimidating?" She fought a laugh. "I'm a woman. I like sex. My life literally revolves around people having sex. I'm not afraid of my sexuality. I embrace it. Men are celebrated all the time for having lots of sex. Nobody will celebrate me liking a lot of sex, so I celebrate myself. Fuck that. I'm not ashamed of that."

I rubbed my hand down my face. "You said sex a lot, and I'm not gonna lie, I'm turned the fuck on right now."

Peyton grinned. It reached her eyes, lighting them right up, and she tapped her fingers against her bare knee. "I know. I can see it."

Apparently, leaning forward didn't actually work.

I sat back instead. I stared at her. At the dark hair that tumbled over her shoulders in loose waves. At the full, pink lips she bit the inside of as she looked right back at me. At the bright eyes that flitted across my body, taking me in much the same was I was her.

Desire swirled through my body.

I wanted to kiss her.

I wanted to walk around the desk. Drag her up. Curl my fingers around the back of her neck. Place my lips on hers until she was dizzy.

I wanted to taste her, to have the sensation of her mouth against mine tingle for the rest of the day.

I got up and walked around the desk. Her gaze followed me, but she didn't try to stop me. She watched, silent, as I knocked her feet from the desk and grabbed her hands.

I pulled her up in one easy sweep. The only reaction she gave was a whimper-gasp when I tugged her body flush against mine.

Now, she blushed. Her deep inhale was obvious and audible. It sent a shiver across my skin. Something so simple, nothing more than touching her, and she reacted as if I was preparing to set her on fire.

Maybe I was. God only knew my skin burned every time she touched me.

"What are you doing?" she breathed. "I'm working."

"You're taking a lunch break."

"I don't have lunch."

"You don't need it." I hooked my finger under her chin and tilted her head up, forcing her eyes to meet mine. "You don't have time to eat, but you have a minute to kiss me."

She shook her head. "Off-limits. I told you that. No kissing. It's too intimate."

"Peyton, I'm going to kiss you. You're going to let me, and you're going to like it." I wasn't leaving any room for discussion—it was fucking well happening. "If I have to go to work with a raging hard-on because all I want to do is flip you over this desk and fuck you 'til you scream, then I'm going to go to work knowing that you're squirming and wet in your thong."

"What if I'm not wearing one?"

"Baby, I don't care if you're fucking commando under that skirt. You're gonna be wet and thinking of me all afternoon no matter what."

She swallowed, her cheeks flushing redder. She might have owned her sexuality, but that didn't mean she was made of stone.

"No kissing," she whispered.

I kissed her anyway. Just one light, fleeting sweep across her soft lips. It was barely there. An accident, almost. Something easily brushed off as leaning forward an inch too far.

She took another deep breath in. Her eyes dropped to my chest. Her breathing was a little quick. A little too loud. A little too forced, as if she were trying to control it but couldn't.

Her body belied her words.

She could talk the talk, but when it came down to it, she couldn't talk herself out of how I affected her. She couldn't even pretend she was a stone-hearted, unaffected woman who had complete control of her body.

And she did. Her body, her fucking beautiful body, was all hers, but she allowed me this. She allowed herself to react to me the way she did. And I would take advantage of it—as long as she let me.

Now was that moment.

As I dipped my face toward hers to test the waters, she tilted hers up. Peyton kissed me, wrapping her arms around my neck. Her body was hard against mine as she briefly took control, establishing herself as the one in charge.

I let her.

I let her kiss me until she let her on her grip.

Until I dug my fingers into her ass cheek and flicked my tongue against her lips, asking her to let me kiss her harder and deeper.

She let me.

My tongue toyed with hers. My cock was hard, pressing against her, and I wished I could roll up her skirt and feel if she was as bothered by this as I was. I wished I could run my fingers over her clit and through her wetness to know how bad she wanted me.

She hated me, but she wanted me.

And I wanted her more than she knew.

"Tonight," I said against her lips. "Come to my place."

"I don't know," she whispered.

"The only reason we're even here is because you're doing this stupid dare. The sooner you fuck me, the sooner you never have to speak to me again."

A tiny laugh left her, and when I released her, she touched her fingers to her swollen lips. "Do you use that line on all the women?"

I smirked. "Nah, you're special. So, tonight?"

She hesitated.

"Come at seven-thirty. Briony will be asleep. You'll just have to not refer to me as a Biblical entity at the top of your voice this time," I teased her.

Peyton pursed her lips. "You're right. The sooner we fuck, the sooner I never have to listen to that kind of egotistical shit again."

I laughed. "So, seven-thirty?"

"On the dot," she replied.

I smiled at her, and just when I thought she was about to say something, her phone rang. The shrill noise cut through the moment, and she self-consciously ran her fingers through her hair, smoothing it down, and reached for it.

I knew that was the cue to leave, so I gently tapped her ass and, when she threw me a dark look, stifled a laugh on my way out.

***

I stared at the almost-bald Barbie.

I had questions. How had she found the scissors, and why had she cut her hair? Not to mention how she'd got it so even. It wasn't a hack job.

All right, so Barbie definitely looked like she'd stuck her fingers in the outlet a few too many times, but it was a pretty round haircut, all in all.

"Why did you cut her hair?" I asked Briony.

My little girl blinked at me. "I didn't. I found her dat way."

"You found her that way."

She emphatically nodded her head. "In duh toybots."

"Why is there hair on your pajamas?"

"It falled out?"

"Okay," I said, crouching down so my eyes were level with hers. "You either found her this way, or you found her with her hair falling out. I'm going to put Barbie down and give you a chance to tell me the truth, or I'm taking Barbie and her friends, and they're going into a box where you can't play with them anymore."

Her eyes widened. "But, Daddy, I got a sore tummy."

Parenting was not for the weak of heart. Or the impatient.

"Sure, you do. Are you going to tell me the truth about her hair?"

Briony fidgeted with the hem of her My Little Pony pajama shirt. "I cutted it," she said in a quiet voice, staring at the floor.

"Where did you get the scissors?"

"Out of duh drawer."

"And what aren't you allowed to get out of the drawer?"

She shifted. "Scissors and knides."

"That's right. Why did you cut her hair?"

"I fort she'd be pretty." She finally looked back up at me. "Daddy, I really do had a tummy ache."

Clearly, we weren't going to finish this without a fake tummy ache. I knew how to pick my battles, and this wasn't one worth fighting about. Besides, she already knew she was wrong.

"Okay. Go lie on the sofa, and I'll vacuum up Barbie's hair." I sighed, chucking her under the chin.

She nodded and climbed up onto it, silently curling onto her side. I gave her a second glance before I left the room and headed upstairs.

No sooner had I stepped foot into her room than I heard the unmistakable sound of retching from downstairs.

I ran down the stairs quicker than I ever had in my life. Briony looked up at me, suddenly deathly pale.

"Daddy," she said scratchily. "I beed sick."

She sure had.

Right into my shoes.

She vomited again. Into the shoes.

This was the shit they didn't warn you about in high school. Screw preaching abstinence—give them a sick toddler and see how they feel about not practicing safe sex after that.

I retrieved a wet cloth and a big mixing bowl from the kitchen, then got to work cleaning up Briony.

And my shoes.

CHAPTER NINE

PEYTON

Nothing killed libido like the lingering smell of vomit. Or your brother accidentally sexting you.

I WASN'T GOING TO BEAT AROUND THE BUSH. I WAS HERE to have sex, and I wasn't going to delay that by wearing pants.

I wanted in, and I wanted out.

In more than one way.

I hadn't been able to get the thought of Elliott kissing me out of my head all damn day. All I could think of was the way he'd grabbed me, how he'd softly tested the water before he'd really kissed me.

Kissing was dangerous.

It was intimate. It had the potential to make someone feel more than they wanted to.

Then again, his smile maybe had that effect, too.

It was hard to reconcile the Elliott of high school with the person he was now. The more I talked to him, the more I realized that he was a million miles away from that person I once knew.

I wanted to let go of the hatred I'd harbored for years, but I didn't have a choice. I had to hold onto it if I wanted to get through these hook-ups and win.

And I did. I wanted to win. I didn't want to fall in love. I liked my life. I liked my freedom and the ability to do whatever the fuck I wanted. I had no desire for anyone to step in and hamper that.

I paid the cab driver and got out of the car. I hadn't bothered to dress up. I'd changed out of the smarter outfit I'd worn when he'd come by my office, but all I'd done was replace it with an equally flattering dress that fitted my bust but flared at my hips.

I felt pretty.

Insert girly twirling here.

I stopped that train of thought before I rolled my eyes at myself and walked up the few steps to the front door. The light was waning, and it was apparently dark enough for a dim security light to come on and illuminate me.

I knocked three times. There was some passionate cussing from the other side of the door and a delay before it opened.

Elliott stood there, shirtless and harried. His sweatpants were low on his hips, allowing me a glimpse at the branded waistband of his boxers.

My favorite part of his outfit was his bright yellow gloves.

I choked back a laugh. "Nice gloves."

He sighed heavily. "Shit. I meant to call you."

"Is this a bad time?"

"No. Yes. It's fine. You're here. Come in." He waved me inside with his gloved hand and stepped to the side.

The mixed smell of vomit and cleaning products hit me with a thump.

"Whoa." I covered my mouse and nose with my hand. "What happened here?"

"Briony cut Barbie's hair and threw up," he threw over his shoulder as he walked into the living room.

I followed him. Reluctantly.

"Ah, the haircut. A right of passage," I said solemnly.

"So, it's normal?" he asked, looking almost relieved.

I nodded. "At least twice more between now and being a tween. I once cut Barbie's hair then used permanent markers to dye her hair black. She had tattoos, too."

He gulped, squeezing a sponge in a bucket of water. "Note to self: hide the Sharpies."

"Good plan. So, she's sick, too?" I asked, hovering in the doorway.

"Yep." He scrubbed at the sofa cushion. "I thought she was using a tummy ache as a ploy to get out of the whole Barbie conversation, but the second I went upstairs to clean her makeshift hair salon, boom. She threw up."

Poor thing. "Is she okay?"

"She's sleeping off a light fever. My mom came over and said it's probably just a fever, and she's gone to get... something from the store to settle her stomach. I can't remember what it was."

"Ginger," I said absently.

"No, she's blonde."

"What?"

"You said ginger, and I said no, she's blonde."

I fought the urge to smile. "No, ginger. Actual ginger. The root?"

He stared at me blankly.

"The cooking ingredient? Looks like a mutant root? It's a natural remedy to ease sickness. My mom used it whenever me and Dom got sick. Mimi, too."

"Oh!" Recognition crossed his face, but it quickly gave way to his stress. "Right. Makes sense. Sorry. I'm not great when she's sick."

Something twanged inside me. Something that had no business twanging.

"I'll go," I offered, taking a step back. He had enough to deal with without worrying about me.

"No," he said a little too quickly. "You don't have to. I haven't eaten yet. I've been busy cleaning up. Stay and eat with me?"

I hesitated. I shouldn't. That was a recipe for disaster.

But, I couldn't say no. He looked exhausted. The lines in his forehead where deep where he had a permanent frown on his face, and his usually shining dark eyes were dull and worried. His lips were downturned, and the decent human being inside me just wanted to give him a hug.

"Sure. But, if I stay, you'll let me help you clean up."

"Absolutely not." He shook his head emphatically. "You don't need to clean up vomit."

"Boy, I wish someone would have told Chloe that after senior homecoming," I muttered, walking past him and putting my purse on the coffee table.

"Why? What happened?"

I clicked my tongue. "Well, after you ruined my night, we went to a party, and she got so drunk she couldn't speak without throwing up. And she did it in my bath."

"After I ruined your night?" He sat back and met my eyes. "Ohh. Shit."

I did nothing but stare at him. Yep. He remembered. How nice of him.

"Thanks for that, by the way. I loved being stood up by my date because you told him rumors he refused to repeat back to me."

"Wait, what?" Elliott's frown grew deeper. "That's not what happened."

"You don't need to lie to me about it. I'm over it."

"You sound it," he drawled. "But that's still not what happened. I never told him anything about you."

I put my hands on my hips. "So, you didn't tell him not to go with me?"

"No, I told him that, but—" He stopped when the front door opened.

"Sorry, darlin'. I had to go to three stores to get the ginger. Three stores!" The familiar voice of his mom filled the room, and she closed the door. "Who the hell runs out of darn ginger?"

Elliott took a deep breath. "Mom…"

"Ridiculous. At least I got my FitBit steps in!" She brightened at that, lifting her left hand to show the blue band around her wrist. "Oh, hello!" she said, catching sight of me with eyes that were the perfect match to Elliott's.

He cleared his throat. "Mom. You remember Peyton."

She placed one perfectly-manicured hand to her chest. "Peyton Austin. Well, I never! Look at you!"

Thank God I'd dressed casually.

"Hi, Mrs. Sloane. It's great to see you."

"Oh, goodness! Mrs. Sloane! Call me Tabby!" She dropped the ginger on the table and enveloped me in a huge hug. She squeezed me so tight I almost couldn't breathe. "How are you, darlin'? Gosh, you're all grown up. Wait, what are you doing here?" She looked at me and Elliott.

"She's here to fix the plumbing, Mom," he said dryly.

She slapped him around the back of his head. "I don't appreciate your attitude, young man."

I hid my smile behind my hand and dipped my chin so neither of them could see the fact I was desperately trying to laugh.

Not that it worked. As Elliott mumbled an apology, his mom caught my eye and winked.

"I assume you were the date from a few days ago?" she asked me.

"Blind date. Chloe and Mellie are jokers," I said a little bitterly.

"Ah. I see someone hasn't apologized for his stunts in high school." She rolled her eyes.

"I'm still here," Elliott said, dropping the sponge into the water. "And we were just talking about that when you barreled in here like a hurricane."

"With ginger to make your daughter feel better," she added with a pointed look. "How is my baby?"

"Sleeping," he answered.

"She vomit up that paracetamol?"

"No. Not yet. Hopefully, she won't."

"Right. I'm going to make this up for her, so when she wakes, you give her some with the other half of that paracetamol dose." She shuffled off into the kitchen, clutching the bag of ginger to her chest.

I couldn't help but smile as she went. She was still the same, blonde-haired, curvy woman I remembered standing in the bleachers every football game.

But this was awkward. Very, very awkward.

"I'm gonna go," I said to Elliott. "This is...weird."

"No. Don't." He stood up and reached for me.

I looked at his hands.

He froze, then pulled off the gloves. He dropped them on the table and touched my upper arms. "Don't. Please. If you go, she's gonna stay and ask me all sorts of stuff about you and why you're here. I need to buy some time to make up a story that doesn't involve us sleeping together to prove your brother wrong," he finished on a whisper.

"This is awkward, Elliott!" I whispered furiously. "I came here to get laid, not catch up with your mom over coffee!"

He snort-laughed. I hit him with a death glare, and he sobered.

"I know. It's not funny. I'm sorry. But, please?" He pushed my bangs out of my eyes. "A favor?"

I folded my arms. "You don't deserve one, but since you're doing me one, I suppose. But I'm not staying long."

"That's fine."

"And you're going to tell me what really happened at homecoming."

He hesitated. His jaw set tensely, but he nodded his agreement. "I was going to before she came in, so you got it."

I stared at him long and hard before his mom walked back in and broke the moment. He dropped his hands from my arms. Tabby looked at us for a moment, clearly unsure whether or not she should speak.

An awkward moment passed before she plastered a bright smile on her face. "So, Peyton. What do you do now? Let's catch up while that ginger boils."

"Oh. I, um, run a hook-up website," I said hesitantly.

"You do? How interesting." She paused and looked at Elliott. "I thought you were signing up to a dating site."

He looked like a deer caught in headlights.

"He did," I said, coming to his rescue. "Chloe and my brother run a dating website. He signed up there, and Chloe forced me into going on a date. She has a sick sense of humor," I added darkly.

Tabby laughed. "Well, what are friends for? Tell me more about this hook-up website of yours."

She looked genuinely interested.

I was going to kill Elliott.

***

Elliott closed the front door and leaned against it.

I slumped back in the armchair and blew out a long breath.

One hour. That was how long his mom had been here catching up with me. Don't get me wrong, she was a lovely woman, but it was still awkward. Not to mention she'd referenced high school several times.

And I was, apparently, the only one who had no idea what genuinely happened at homecoming. Which probably meant I didn't know why he stood me up or egged my car, either.

Elliott walked in from the kitchen with a glass of wine and a beer. He handed me the wine and sat on the dry end of the sofa.

I looked at his beer.

He waved it. "Stressed. I ordered Dominos on the app. They said fifteen minutes. Pepperoni, right?"

"Yeah," I said slowly. "Was that a lucky guess, or…?"

"It was your favorite in high school before you hated me. How often do people change their pizza preferences?"

"I don't know. Is that trivia?"

"Rhetorical." His lips tugged to the side. "But it was also kind of a lucky guess."

At least he was honest.

"Should we talk about high school before or after food?" I asked.

"Whenever you want to."

"How pissed off am I going to be?"

He laughed. "Probably not as pissed as you are believing the bullshit story Todd fed you."

I raised my eyebrows. "We'll see. Depends if I believe you or not."

"Hey, I have no reason to lie to you, Peyton. If you'd ever bothered to listen to me when we were in school, you'd know that."

"What does that mean?"

"After junior prom, I tried to explain why I wasn't there. You never spoke to me again."

"Because you humiliated me!" I took a deep breath. That had come out a little shriller than I'd planned. "You humiliated me," I said again, this time softer. "Everyone knew we were supposed to go to prom together, then you never showed up. Did you expect me to just stop and forgive you?"

"No. I never expected you to forgive me. I don't even expect you to now. But I expected you to listen to me when I wanted to tell you why."

"Yeah, well, I was a pissy teenage girl," I snapped.

"And now you're a pissy grown woman who sounds like she still won't listen."

I glared at him. He was right, but I was going to listen because I wanted to know. His reign of terror over my last year of high school had begun the night of junior prom, and I had a feeling everything was directly linked to that night.

After ten years, I'd finally have the answer to why he stood me up and had me stood up only months later.

At least, I was going to. Until the warbling cry of "Daddy!" coincided with the deafening echo of the doorbell ringing.

CHAPTER TEN

PEYTON

The truth was a bitch. No, really. She was like that one ex who tells you they're still in love with you on your wedding day. (Looking at you, Rachel Green.)

"CAN YOU ANSWER THE DOOR?" ELLIOTT ASKED ME, putting down his beer and jumping up. He didn't wait for me to answer before he ran upstairs to where Briony was yelling for him, now crying.

"Sure," I muttered to myself. I set my wine on the coffee table and went to answer the door. The doorbell rang again seconds before I opened it, and I stared flatly at the delivery guy.

"Two large pizzas," he said in a dull drawl.

"Thanks." I took them and shut the door with as much enthusiasm as he'd handed me the boxes. I put the boxes on the table as the sound of water running reached my ears.

The scent of the pizzas was driving me crazy. My mouth watered at the rich tomatoey, cheesy scent.

Would it be rude to eat it?

Yes.

No.

Yes.

Ugh. Now, I was hungry. In fact, I didn't even know why I was here. Briony clearly needed Elliott, so me staying was futile. Even though I wasn't necessarily a kid kind of person, I'd done my fair share of babysitting in both high school and college.

Sick kids equaled clingy kids. As they should.

I should have left earlier. I knew it was the right choice.

Hell, I still think I should have walked out the moment I walked into the restaurant.

I picked up my purse and wandered into the hall, where I hesitated. I couldn't leave without saying goodbye, could I?

Selfishly, I still needed Elliott.

I was a horrible person. A horrible, horrible person.

I put my purse down by the front door and quietly made my way upstairs. The gentle sound of his voice shushing tiny, helpless cries tugged at my heartstrings, and I had to take a deep breath before I could go up the last few stairs.

"Hey, princess, it's okay," I heard him say softly. "It doesn't matter. I can change your bed. You want the pony sheets or the princess ones?"

"Cindewella," she sniffed.

What was I doing here? I should have just gone. Left a note. Texted him.

Texting sounded good...

"Okay, let me get that. Give me two seconds." I turned to walk down the stairs right as he stepped out of the bathroom.

His eyes caught mine before I could dart away and get away from Dad Elliott. "Peyton?"

I cocked a thumb awkwardly. "I was, uh...I should go."

He nodded, understanding clouding his eyes. "I get it. But, could you just...actually, never mind. It's fine."

Don't ask. Don't ask.

"What?" I asked.

Idiot.

"It's fine," he replied.

"No, what?"

He said nothing.

"Elliott Daniel Sloane!"

"Jesus." He ran his hand through his hair. "Only my mother uses my middle name."

I hit him with a look she'd probably be damn well proud of.

"Fine." He dropped his hand with vigor. "Could you just watch Bri for a minute? She was a little sick, and I have to change her bed sheets. She's in the bath, or I wouldn't ask. It went in her hair, and..." He trailed off with a shudder.

Oh. Oh, damn.

"Uh."

Think fast, Peyton. Think fast!

"Sure," was what came out of my mouth. I'd done it before, and I could do it again. Hell, I'd once bathed two three-year-old boys in a college babysitting stint. They'd bathed me, too.

"Are you sure?"

"I'm sure. I promise. Go change her bed. I can watch her."

He shot me the most grateful look I'd ever been on the end of and darted back into the bathroom. "Bri, Daddy's friend is going to watch you while I change your bed, okay? I'll be two minutes."

"Okay," she whispered.

I looked at him, then slipped into the bathroom. It wasn't huge. Just big enough that I could sit on the toilet to watch Briony in the water.

She was beautiful.

Sure, her blonde hair was damp with sweat, and she was pale, but there was no denying that she was one of the prettiest kids I'd ever seen. She had the biggest eyes, even if they were saddened by her tummy ache. The most perfect little button nose and ribbon lips finished off her baby features.

"Hi," I said softly.

She looked up at me. "Hi," she whispered. "Are you Peydon?"

I put down the toilet seat and perched on the edge of it. "I am. Are you Briony?"

A tiny smile twitched at her lips. "I am. And I sick."

"I know. Your daddy said. How do you feel, sweetie?"

"My tummy hurts. And I gotted sick in my hair." She picked up a chunk of her blonde hair and looked at it. Immediately, she wrinkled up her face and dropped it. "I need a shampoo."

I looked at the bottle that had a princess on the side. The word "shampoo" was in big, bold letters, and Briony reached for it. She unscrewed the top and squeezed the bottle. Bright blue gel landed in her palm with a quiet plop.

"Oh—you need to make your hair wet first," I said before she could put the shampoo on her hair. "Here. Let me help you. Turn around."

I got up and pulled the showerhead down from its holder. Starting the water, I carefully tested the temperature of the water as she hummed along to a tune I didn't recognize.

"Is this too hot?" I asked.

She stuck her hand under the stream of water. "Good."

"Okay, good. Tilt your head back. I don't want to get it in your eyes."

Briony leaned her head so far back I thought she might topple backward. She closed her eyes and even put her hand over them to protect them. I couldn't help the smile that stretched over my face as I brought the shower head close to her head.

She was adorable.

I took extra care to wash her hair. She held the showerhead while I gently worked the shampoo into her hair and handed it back so I could rinse it.

"'Ditioner, too?" she asked when I pulled the showerhead away.

"Sure."

She reached forward and picked up another brightly-colored bottle, then handed it to me and took the shower head. I ran the conditioner through her hair, then did the rinse thing again.

"There you go. All done." I shut off the water, replaced the shower head, and squeezed the extra water out of her hair.

She spun around in the tub and smiled up at me with as much brightness as a kid with the stomach flu could muster. It was more than I expected—but, then again, sometimes a good hair wash could do wonders.

"Fank you," she said with a tiny lisp.

I sat back on the toilet with a smile. "You're very welcome."

She dropped her head and looked at the mermaid toy she had in her hand. The bright red hair gave it away as Ariel, even if she was completely naked.

Ah. She cut Barbie's hair, and her doll was naked. She was a classic little girl.

That made me smile, too.

"Are you all done?" Elliott leaned against the doorframe and looked at us both. "Hey! Did you wash your hair all by yourself?"

"No! Silly Daddy. Peydon did it."

Pey*d*on.

That was adorable.

"She do it best than you." She grinned at him. "I ready to ged out now."

"Better than me?" Elliott feigned shock as he pulled a pink towel from a bar on the wall. "Careful on your steps."

Briony stood up and almost rolled over the side of the tub onto the plastic kids steps on the floor. She almost slipped on the wet plastic but managed to stay upright until Elliott wrapped her in the fluffy towel and scooped her up.

"How's your tummy feel?" he asked.

I followed him out of the bathroom.

"Bedder. I tired, Daddy."

I caught his eye and motioned to go downstairs. He smiled and nodded, and I left him to dry her and change her.

The pizza boxes drew my attention instantly.

I no longer cared if it was rude. I could feel my mind gearing up to go a million miles an hour, so I checked both pizza boxes and grabbed mine, then sat down on the sofa.

The wet cushion.

I squealed and jumped up, almost dropping the pizza box as the wetness went through the thin material of my dress. I quickly darted over the room to the safety of the armchair and sat in it.

Then tugged up my dress so I didn't have to sit on the damp material.

What? Nobody wants their tushy to be wet.

I took a bite of the pizza slice.

Why was I here? What was I doing? Shouldn't I have left by now?

What had possessed me to wash Briony's hair? To do something so gentle to such a beautiful kid who was born to someone I hated.

Or... did I? Hate him?

Not only was my entire perception of junior prom onward apparently misconstrued, but seeing him with his little girl?

Excuse you, ovaries.

You don't get to go boom. You get to slam your whore legs shut and fry those eggs instead of releasing them.

Seeing him with Briony was dangerous. He was so soft, so gentle. So tanned against her paler skin. They were night and day. He was dark where she was light, and she was tiny where he was large.

He should not have been able to be so gentle with her. And, honestly, to my annoyance, the hottest thing I'd seen in a long time was him picking up his sick toddler while she was wrapped in a hot pink towel.

How was I ever supposed to scratch that out of my mind?

Oh. That's right. I wasn't.

I slammed the pizza crust into the box and snatched up another piece, only to tear off a bite. I was almost a Neanderthal, and this was almost certainly pizza abuse. No pizza deserved to be eaten by a pack of wild dogs.

Which was how my annoyance was making me eat this.

Like a savage.

A sexually-frustrated, emotionally confused savage.

Ugh. I ripped off another piece of pizza and chewed.

It was cold. Thank God it was pizza. It was, after all, one of the only things that tasted good cold.

Pizza, best served cold. Right up there with revenge.

Ahh, revenge…

Did I have a plot for revenge? Was revenge on the cards? Was revenge anything I had justification for?

This sucked.

Had I been a typical woman and held a grudge for ten years for no reason?

Man, that was not a slice of humble pie I wanted to eat. I bet it wouldn't taste as good as this pizza.

I finished the second slice. I dropped the crust on top of the other and grabbed the third slice. I was halfway through it when the light dimmed drastically.

Looking up, I saw the reason why. Elliott was filling the entire doorway, and apparently, it'd gotten dark during my thinking session.

"It's dark," he said, confirming my suspicions.

"I was hungry," I said through a mouthful of pizza. "Sorry."

He stared at me for a second, then laughed as he twisted the dial to turn the lights up to full brightness. "Don't worry. Is it really cold?"

I nodded solemnly, taking another bite.

"Hey. Cold Dominos is the best. Don't look so sad."

Man. He was a couple conversations away from having the potential to be my soulmate.

Shut up. I took pizza seriously.

I took yet another bite. I didn't want to speak. I wanted to eat. I was still hungry. I was hungry and torn and frustrated.

So, I ate.

I nibbled down to the crust of the third piece of pizza before I lost my appetite. I dropped that, too, then stared at the rest of the pizza.

Out of the corner of my eye, I saw Elliott put down his second slice.

"You know," he said, "You didn't have to do what you did."

"What did I do?" I closed the box and leaned over to put it on the table.

"Washing Bri's hair."

I shrugged a shoulder. "She was going to try to do it with her hair dry. That wouldn't have worked. I was helping her."

His lips twitched. "Sure. Thank you."

"It's no big deal." I smiled, even though I felt a little awkward. It had been a spontaneous decision, and I wasn't sure how I felt about being that nice.

"So...Did you want to finish what we started?"

I paused, staring at him.

"High school conversation," he said slowly, a grin stretching across his face.

"I don't know why you're grinning. It makes me want to punch myself in the face. And you, for that matter." My expression had to be the total opposite of his.

"I'm not smiling about high school. I'm smiling because you looked, for a minute, like you thought I was talking about something else."

"Yeah, well, we need to get on with finishing that, too," I muttered. I sighed and adjusted how I was sitting in the chair. "Fine. You were going to tell me what happened at homecoming?"

Elliott shifted, almost uncomfortably. "Actually, I need to start with prom."

I leaned back and folded my arms across my chest. I even tapped my foot for good measure. This didn't sound good, and I wasn't sure I actually wanted to hear it anymore.

"I didn't stand you up deliberately," he started. "About an hour before I was going to leave, my mom got a call from the hospital that'd been treating my grandmother. She'd had a stroke that afternoon and died."

Oh my god.

"She threw me into the car still wearing my suit. I didn't even have time to grab my phone to tell you I wouldn't be there." He ran his hand through his hair. "And then, you wouldn't listen to me. I thought you might be coming around when your car got egged."

I swallowed. "By you."

He shook his head. "I had nothing to do with it. I knew you thought I did, and that's why I pretty much gave up trying to explain to you what happened."

"There was a note on my windshield signed by you," I told him. "Even the writing was similar."

"I swear to you, Peyton, it wasn't me. I was trying to make it up to you—why would I do something to hurt you when you were already mad at me?"

I didn't say anything. I didn't know what to think anymore.

"As for homecoming...I told Todd I needed a favor. He was trying to get on the football team, so I told him that if he decided not to take you to homecoming so that I could, I'd talk to the coach about him." Elliott rubbed his hand across his mouth. "He agreed."

"So? What happened?"

"I got sick. I wasn't even in school that day, and I didn't have your number. You changed it after prom, and as far as I knew, told every person in our year that if they ever gave me your number that you'd make their life a living hell."

I shifted awkwardly. "Only hypothetically."

"Well, apparently, you were serious enough that they all believed you." His lips twitched to the side. "To be honest, if you told me that, I'd have believed you, too."

Shrugging one shoulder, I said, "So, what you're telling me is that I've hated you for years for no reason?"

"Maybe. Maybe not. I could have done more to make you listen. Whether I meant to or not, I hurt you, and I don't think I ever took responsibility for that."

"It wasn't your fault, though," I said quietly. "You had no control over the situation, and I was a stubborn bitch." Some things didn't change. "I don't—I don't know how I feel about this."

I knew staying was a bad idea.

When would I learn to listen to my gut?

Elliott's dark gaze was steady on me, but I saw no judgment. I saw no anger or frustration from him.

In fact, his gaze was almost reserved. Like he was holding in any emotions except for the hint of regret that had tinged all his words.

I knew one thing. I couldn't be here right now. It was such a stupid thing, but I was angry. I was furious.

At myself.

At teenage Peyton.

And more than anything, I needed to process.

"I have to go," I said, standing up. I grabbed my purse from the table, almost knocking over the wine glass in the process, and walked toward the door.

"Peyton…" He followed me with silent footsteps.

I turned and looked at him, keeping my hand on the doorknob. "I have to process this, Elliott. I don't know how I feel about this or how I'm supposed to."

"You have a habit of ignoring me when I do—or say—something you don't like." Hurt flashed in his eyes for a split second.

A hurt I felt clenching in my stomach.

"I'm not the person I was in high school. Just like you aren't. I'm not running away, but you have to understand that for the last ten years, I thought you hurt me deliberately." Admitting that wasn't easy, and now, the hurt was spreading through my body. "To find out that you didn't, that you were in your own kind of pain and I never knew because I ignored you is something I need to think over. I need to process everything you just told me, because believe it or not, this changes everything."

He looked me in the eye, then reached up and pushed my bangs from my eyes. He said nothing, but he didn't need to. His silence said more than he ever could.

I opened the door and walked out without another word. I didn't have a cab or any way to get home, but I didn't care right now.

I just walked.

And walked.

And walked.

Until I reached one of the most familiar-to-me buildings in this city.

I knocked on the door, knowing I was about to get my ass chewed out for waking her up.

The windows on the door gave way to a wavy reflection, illuminated by the lights in the hallway. After a couple of clicks and the tell-tale tick of the key turning, the door opened.

Mimi looked at me as if she wanted to kill me. She opened her mouth to speak, but whatever she was going to say never came out. Instead, her expression softened, the tired frustration in her eyes quickly giving way to love.

"I don't want to talk about it right now," I said quietly. "But can I stay with you tonight?"

"Oh, darlin'." She pulled me to her and hugged me tightly, stroking my hair and kissing it. "You always can. Come on in here. Let me get you hot cocoa and make your bed for you."

"I can make the bed," I said as she dragged me inside. "I woke you up. I'm sorry."

"Don't you dare be sorry," she scolded me. "You're sad. I'm the person you come to when you're sad. So, I'm gonna make you hot cocoa, and you're gonna sit down while I get your bed done. Got it?"

I nodded. "I got it."

I followed her into the kitchen where she bustled about to make the cocoa. From scratch.

I must have looked really fucking miserable. Cocoa from scratch was a rare thing, and almost always happened if someone had died.

And, in a way, something had died.

But I couldn't think about it. Just twenty minutes ago I'd left Elliott at his door with the declaration that I needed to process, and here I was, ignoring it. Like I was in denial.

"Mimi?"

"Yes, darlin'?"

"What would you do if you got information that had the potential to not only change what you've believed for ten years, but also made you realize you were wrong and could change everything you think you know right now?"

"That's a loaded question, ain't it?" She poured the cocoa from the pot into a giant Piglet mug. She put the pot in the sink, then slid me the mug across the table.

"I guess that would depend on how much it would change my life."

"Probably a lot," I admitted.

"Then, I would take all the time I needed to really think it through."

"How much is too much time? Because I don't want to think about it right now."

"As much as you need, sugar." She reached over and squeezed my hand. "And when I was done thinkin' about it, I'd go to the people who would understand the situation the best."

Well, that part was easy.

"Thanks, Mimi. Do you mind if I take this up to bed?"

"Not at all. I have to go make it, though."

"I've got it. Really. Go back to bed. And thank you."

Mimi rounded the table and wrapped me in yet another hug. She held onto me a little tighter and a little longer than she had at the door, and she kissed the top of my head twice before releasing me.

"Goodnight, darlin'. I'll make you waffles in the morning." A third kiss accompanied that, and I smiled.

"That sounds perfect. Goodnight, Mimi."

CHAPTER ELEVEN

ELLIOTT

There's always a right and wrong time for truth. Even when it's the right time, chances are, life is gonna fuck you up the ass without lube anyway.

ONE HOUR. IT'D BEEN ONE HOUR SINCE PEYTON HAD LEFT, looking dazed and confused and angry. I'd been sitting here in silence the entire time, a part of me wishing I could have chased her down the street.

Why had I told her the truth? Sure, I'd fought for months to do that in school, but this wasn't school anymore. It didn't matter.

She could have quite easily hate-fucked me two more times, then disappeared out of my life. The likelihood of our paths ever crossing again was incredibly low, because we'd likely have plans in place to avoid each other.

Now, she knew. She knew I hadn't been a raging asshole. That even though I'd hurt her, I hadn't had control over those situations.

I'd never wanted to.

Fuck, I'd wanted her to fall in love with me, not want to kill me on sight.

And now? Now, she knew, and I had no time to fall in love.

Not that she would. I had baggage, more than she knew about, and our lives were polar opposites. Never mind that she had a hidden soft side that made her wash the hair of a sick three-year-old. Never mind that her smile sent a shiver down my spine every time I got a glimpse of a genuine one.

Never mind that the look in her eyes before she'd left had punched me straight in the gut.

Peyton was a tornado in a teacup. A wild, beautiful force of nature ready to forge a path for herself, no matter who or what was in her way.

I wouldn't be the one who'd make her change her course.

I knew, sitting here, that I needed to text her. To apologize for telling her and put an end to this experiment.

Telling her the truth about high school had changed everything. She'd been right when she said that. I could already see that she'd taken blame for some of it, when none of it had been her fault.

Had she been stubborn? Ignorant? Pig-headed?

Yes. One hundred percent, there was no doubt about that.

But she hadn't been wrong, either. We were seventeen. She'd reacted based on what she knew, and she just happened to have a fiery, angry streak that, if you were unlucky, could unleash the fires of hell on you if you pissed her off.

In that respect, I'd been lucky. Even if I now wished she'd screamed at me, if only so I'd been able to tell her the truth.

There was no way she'd ever know about my grandmother, either. I didn't tell anyone. It wouldn't have changed anything, and if she'd ever found out, I believe it wouldn't have changed anything.

Not only had she been almost intolerably stubborn back then—as she was now—she'd been proud. Too proud. And one of the things I'd done to her was damaged that pride. I'd embarrassed her in front of our entire year. Her friends, her family, total strangers.

Everyone had known I'd asked her to prom. She'd been the It Girl, after all. She'd been untouchable, just because of how she handled herself.

And in one second, I'd inadvertently destroyed a part of that.

No. Her finding out the truth from anyone else wouldn't have made a difference. She would have been too embarrassed by her own stubbornness to apologize for ignoring me.

Not that it mattered.

I'd long forgotten the end of school. I'd been busy, after all, but seeing her brought it all back.

I'd liked her. Really liked her. If I'd been asked back then, maybe I'd have said that she was The One in the way all idiot teens thought they'd found The One.

She'd been out of my life so long, and in a city like New Orleans, I never imagined she'd ever find her way back into it. Or that I'd find my way into hers.

Especially since I had Briony. She was the gamechanger in this, but she was my daughter. I already had one fight on my hands.

As deflated as I felt, as low as my stomach had dropped at the sound of the door shutting behind Peyton, I didn't know if I had the ability to take on another.

Which was stupid, because really, there was nothing to fight for.

There was no relationship. There were barely any feelings. All there was, was the lingering cloud of the past we shared.

One that had been fraught with naïve decisions, immature actions, and unfortunate circumstances.

Certainly nothing real.

She owned a hook-up website and reveled in her freedom.

I had a daughter and was braced for the fight of my life.

Oil and water.

We were oil and water, and if she was going to go through with this experiment, it needed to be done as soon as possible, so we could return to our normal lives.

Before one of us did something really stupid.

CHAPTER TWELVE

PEYTON

Fuck adulting. Fuck feelings. Fuck the donut store that runs out of my favorite donuts.
Fuck the donut store in particular.

I WAS BITTER AND I WAS ANGRY.

It was comparable to that moment in sex where the guy comes, and you don't. We'd all been there, some of us, unfortunately, more than others. It was also up there with the realization that you've watched too much porn because you're disappointed that your plumber isn't young and hot but married and a grandfather.

Just me?

Moving on.

Yes. I was bitter and I was angry.

Sleeping and Mimi's waffles hadn't lessened the initial burst of anger that had slammed into me at Elliott's admission.

I hated myself. Dramatic, but that was how I felt right now. He'd lost his grandma, and I'd just been too damn stubborn and prideful to listen to when he tried to explain to me.

More to the point, I'd taken the hurt and ran with it.

I hadn't ever thought about whether or not him standing me up was in his nature. If it was something a nice guy would do without reason.

"Well, shit," Chloe said when I was done giving the recap.

Mellie whistled low. "Now, what?"

"Now, we fucked up," Chloe muttered.

"That, too."

I rolled my eyes. "That's kind of the theme here." I leaned forward on my desk, almost knocking over my coffee. "Ugh, you guys. You're assholes. Why did you match me with him? Can I blame you for this?"

"You can try, but give it ten years, and you'll be all pissed off again." Chloe sipped from her drink. "What are you most mad about?"

I rolled my head to the side and looked at them. "Myself."

Mellie raised her eyebrows so high they disappeared beneath her bangs. "Are you admitting you were...wrong?"

Wow. My friends knew how to kick a girl when she was down.

"No. I'm considering the fact I may have been too stubborn, but not wrong." I wasn't going to give them that much satisfaction.

They were my best friends. They didn't need satisfaction today. They needed to feel my pain. That was how friendship worked.

I mean, when I was seven, I deliberately got chicken pox so I could still go to Chloe's house.

If I could get pox for her, they could do this for me.

"Well," Chloe said, "As a rule, you're always stubborn."

"No, I'm not," I replied. "I take breaks on Wednesdays."

"Peyt." Mellie fought a laugh. "Anyone who responds to, "you're stubborn" with a denial, is a stubborn piece of ass."

"No, they're—" I caught myself before I proved her point further. "You're supposed to be here to help me. I'm in a crisis."

"Running out of toilet paper is a crisis to you."

"Have you ever sat on the toilet to poop, then ran out of toilet paper while your phone rings?" I raised an eyebrow. "I don't want to speak to someone when I'm pooping. I want Buzzfeed to tell me what breed of cat I'll be in my next life."

"Can you link me to that?" Chloe asked.

Mellie shot her an unamused look. "Chloe."

"What? I poop, too."

"Can we get back to me?" I sat up and waved my arms. "You guys, this is a nightmare. This isn't how this was supposed to go. We had a plan. Go in, get laid three times, bank five hundred dollars. Not go in, meet high school nemesis, wash his sick kid's hair, find out you hated him for no reason, and get fucked."

Mellie shrugged. "Getting fucked was always the plan."

"Literally. Not metaphorically." I slumped forward again and ran both hands through my hair. "This is a disaster. What do I do? Dom knows about Elliott. He knows we slept together. I can't back out now. But how can I have sex with him knowing my hate was unjustified? Oh, God. I need Mardi Gras back so I can get blind drunk and sleep with a tourist."

Chloe cough-snorted, then leaned over to Mellie. "Hey, Mel. Can you Google the price of a train ticket to Pityville for an adult?"

I flipped her the bird. "Seriously. Think about it like this. I've hated him for ten years because of what he did to me—or what I thought he did. He didn't do it. The only reason I never found out was because I was stubborn as hell and wouldn't listen to him when he wanted to explain. I literally hurt myself because I was so up myself.

"Sixty seconds. That's all he would have needed to tell me the truth, and I couldn't set aside how I felt for one fucking minute to listen to him. He lost his grandmother, and I had a giant stick up my ass."

My best friends looked at me. They both just sat deathly still, their eyes on me. There was sympathy in them, but there was also the one thing I didn't have.

The outside perspective.

Of being the people who saw everything in a way I never could, because my feelings had always clouded my judgment.

"And he really, really hurt you," Mellie said softly after a moment of silence. "Peyt, you didn't know. You acted based on the information you had available to you and—"

"I had it available. I chose not to listen to it."

"We were kids!" Chloe said a little too loud. She must have realized she almost yelled because she took a deep breath and held up her hands. "We were kids. We were seventeen, for fuck's sake. We were young. We were stupid. We were immature. Don't hate yourself for what you did then."

"I hate myself for sleeping with Daniel Wynn," Mellie offered.

"And so you should," Chloe replied. "But that was a sober, educated, fully-informed choice that is not helpful right now."

Despite it all, I smiled.

Actually, it was helpful. Because for a moment, I didn't hate myself for the choice I'd made.

I remembered just how freaking dumb we were in high school. How we made decisions on the fly with nothing more than emotions and hormones to guide us.

I blamed algebra for that. My days were so full of Y trying to find his X that I couldn't focus on anything else.

Mostly because I am not a math girl.

"Oh, man," I said, shaking my head. "What am I supposed to do now?"

Mellie sighed. "Do you have a multiple-choice option?"

"Yes. Whine, cry, get drunk, masturbate."

"So…A normal menstrual cycle for you, then," Chloe offered with a grin.

"I…" I paused. "Yeah. Pretty much." I let out a long breath and sat back in my chair, pulling my take-out coffee off the coaster toward me. "I don't know what I'm supposed to do. I'm in trouble. He's not the person I thought he was in high school. Or maybe he is because apparently, I didn't know who he was."

Neither of them said anything, again. We all sat, none of us making eye contact. Mellie stared at my computer, Chloe chewed her thumbnail and stared at the awkward heart canvases that were on my wall.

Awkward because one looked like a penis... and another like a vagina. The other was a legit heart.

Pretty much.

There were no answers. None.

I didn't know how to deal with this, and that was beyond comprehension for me. I'd never been in a situation I couldn't control.

At least not one that had blindsided me the way this one had.

"I think you need to talk to him," Chloe said. "The only way you'll figure this all out is if you both talk it through."

I hated talking. I wasn't a talker. I was a doer.

"Great. That can't possibly go wrong," I muttered, grabbing my phone. I pulled up my messages, then our text chain, and tapped the reply box.

Me: *We need to talk. Tonight.*

His response was swift.

Elliott: *We do. Mom is coming to my house to watch B. At yours?*
Me: *Whenever you're ready.*
Elliott: *I'll put B to bed then come over. I'll text you when I'm leaving.*
Me: *K.*

If I lost this bet because I talked to him, I was going to book a flight the hell away from this planet. I bet Elon Musk would be able to hook a girl up.

If only he could have delayed the Tesla thing. I'd have been more than happy to travel through space in his car.

More than that, this situation had turned me into the kind of person I hated most.

The "k" person.

Ugh.

***

I was out of wine and donuts.

My foot was dancing to an imaginary beat. The nervous taps were the only sound in the room as I read through the application of a single mom who wanted to get out more now her son was getting older.

I wasn't the person she was after, I could tell, so I wrote her a very sweet email explaining that Stupid Cupid could probably help her more.

It happened more often than people would think. They email me for no-strings, but the undertone of their email said they wanted strings. They didn't just want sex—they wanted the cuddling that came after.

I hadn't minored in psychology for nothing.

The fact the professor had been hot was a bonus.

All right. I minored because of the professor. It was like eighteen-year-old Peyton knew I'd need the life skills one day.

And it was really, really handy when it came to avoiding the assholes. Except my friends.

And myself.

I stared up at the blank TV screen on the other side of my office. I needed to put *Friends* on it or something, but I couldn't stand the angst levels. Right now, I just wanted a montage of Joey with food or Pheobe's comments.

None of the Ross and Rachel bullshit. And that was a lot of bullshit.

I sighed and leaned back in my chair. My email pinged with three more notifications, but they were just submissions from guys. I'd looked at approximately eighty different dicks today, and I was done with that.

I shut the laptop.

Waiting for Elliott was driving me insane. I was antsy and anxious—I had no idea how this conversation was going to do, and more than anything, I was afraid of how it would go.

I was afraid it would go well. That would make proving my brother wrong impossible.

This whole idea had been a stupid one from the start.

Why was I so obsessed with the idea of proving him wrong? Surely I could just tell Elliott I was done and tell Dom to go and fuck himself.

I picked up my phone. That was what I was going to do. I was going to put an end to the experiment that was causing me unnecessary stress.

I was Peyton Austin. I didn't get stressed. I was dramatic, but not prone to stress.

Yet, here I was, more stressed than I'd ever been in my life.

This was why people used my website to hook up without strings. Emotions were of the devil.

And the devil was a whore.

I opened my phone and pulled up my messages with Elliott for the second time today. My thumb tapped the box just as a bubble popped up on his side of the screen.

Elliott: *I think your doorbell is broken.*

It was. But how did he—

Shit. He was here already.

I dropped my phone like it was burning me and ran downstairs. Thankfully, I was barefoot, so I wasn't slipping on the floor. If I were Mellie, she'd have gone down the stairs on her ass.

I hesitated before I opened the door. I'd rushed down here as if a hungry werewolf was on my heels, and now I was frozen like the big chicken I was.

Dear God. Only a few days ago I'd had his dick in my mouth, and now I couldn't open the door to him.

I was not good at being a good adult.

"Peyton, I heard you in there. Open the door before your neighbors call the cops on me." Laughter laced his tone.

"But if they call the cops, I won't have to open it." I wasn't supposed to say that out loud. Crap.

He laughed. "You're the one who said we need to talk. Let me in."

Well, there it was. I had no choice.

Welcome to Hell, Peyton.

I ran my hand through my hair as I opened the door. Chewing the inside of my cheek, I met his eyes. "Hey."

"Hey." He was leaning against the doorframe. His hands were tucked into the pockets of his light-blue jeans, and his white t-shirt was a little dirty on the sleeve.

"You know you've got a mark on your shirt?"

"I have a child. I'm more surprised if I leave the house without anything on my shirt."

"Fair enough. Um, come in?" I walked backward, almost tripping over my purse where I'd left it on the floor.

"How was your day?" Elliott asked, tinging the air with the awkwardness of small talk.

"Long. Yours? Do you want coffee?" I shuffled into the kitchen. Why were my palms sweating?

What was this madness?

I wiped my hands on my butt and turned on the coffee machine. "Coffee?"

"You already asked me that." His lips twitched up to the side. "Peyton...Are you nervous?"

"I don't know what you're talking about." I pulled two mugs down from the cupboard and set them on the side. "You didn't answer, that's all, so I repeated myself."

"You're a dreadful liar."

"Actually, I'm a very good liar."

"All right, that wasn't such a bad lie."

I shot a withering look over my shoulder and replaced the pod in the coffee machine.

"I don't need a coffee. I'm good. But thank you."

"Oh. Okay." I didn't want one either. I just wanted to do something with my hands.

Needed something to do with my hands.

"Peyton." His voice was lower but closer, and when I turned around, he was right there. His body was so perfectly muscled that he took up all my immediate personal space, and the scent of sawdust and spring air filled my senses.

He smelled like perfection.

I never wanted to smell it again.

"Stop," he said quietly. "We have to talk about this, and you know it, or you wouldn't have sent me that text."

I did know it. I didn't have to like it, but I knew it.

"We can small talk over coffee, but that's not me, and that's not you, so let's cut that off right away and get right to it." His eyes settled on mine, and I couldn't decipher how he felt just from looking at him.

"Okay, fine," I said, shrugging a shoulder. "Let's go sit and talk about this."

"Lets. In a second, though."

"Why not right now? You just said—"

He cut me off with a kiss. One that had his hand curling around the back of my neck and shivers shooting down my spine. It was slow and gentle, his lips moving with mine as if he was committing my mouth to memory.

"What was that?" I asked when he stopped.

Elliott met my eyes and took a deep breath. "When this conversation is over, I might not get to do that again. And I wanted to make sure I could kiss you one more time."

I swallowed. Hard. I wasn't expecting him to say that.

Worse? I didn't know if I wanted that to be the last time he kissed me.

This was dangerous territory right here.

"Right. Well, um. Let's talk?" Why was I incapable of not just saying it? Why did I keep asking him things?

He nodded. "Let's talk."

I skirted around him and led him toward the living room. We both took a seat on my sofa, and I tucked my feet under my butt.

Silence.

I didn't know what to say. I had so many things I wanted to, I think, but none of them seemed like they were the right thing.

Did I apologize for ignoring him? Did I acknowledge what he'd told me? Did I ask him why he'd told me?

Did I stop thinking and grow a fucking pair?

CHAPTER THIRTEEN

ELLIOTT

*Not everything in life is worth it.
Honesty. Stress. Staying up all night.
Answering the phone...*

SHE WOULDN'T LOOK AT ME.

I could see it all rolling around in her head, and it was obvious that she couldn't find the words. I waited another minute for her to say something before I finally gave in and killed the silence between us.

"I'm sorry if I upset you last night."

She jerked her head up and met my eyes. "I wasn't upset. I was shocked."

If emotional walls were real, there would have been a deafening bang as hers went up so fast it broke the fucking sound barrier.

"You looked like I told you I just killed your puppy," I said. "If that was shocked, then I'll be damned."

"I wasn't upset," she repeated, lying through her teeth. "I just needed to get away and process it all."

She was so full of shit.

"Did you?" I'd play along. For now.

"Mostly. I realized I was stupid to not listen to you."

That sounded like it was the closest to an apology I'd ever get.

I didn't get it. She'd looked as if I'd gutted her when she left last night, and when I'd gotten here just minutes ago, it'd been obvious she'd wanted to be anywhere but here.

Now, she'd closed off.

And that pissed me off.

"Oh," I said flatly. "I could have told you that ten years ago."

Her blue gaze was cutting. "No, you couldn't have. I wasn't listening to you back then."

I almost laughed, but I forced myself not to. I didn't want to laugh at her. I didn't want her to be sarcastic—I wanted her to be fucking real and honest.

Something I wasn't sure she was capable of.

"Is that all we're saying, then? That you realized you were stupid?" I asked.

"I'm sorry I didn't listen," she said, a little more honest this time. "I don't know if it would have made a difference, but I wish I had."

"It would have." I believed that. It would have changed a lot of things. "If we're done, I'm gonna go."

She did a double-take, blinking quickly at me. "You're leaving?"

"I have stuff to do, Peyton. I have laundry to wash. I have to get a stain out of the back of a princess dress. I have to clean up after a tiny human. Not to mention eat, shower, and make sure there are bananas, because all hell will break loose tomorrow if there aren't. Check calls and emails in case my lawyer has contacted me." I stood up and, after a couple of steps away from her, turned and looked at her. "I have a million things to do that don't involve listening to you lie to me."

"Lie to you?" There was a creak as she got up and followed me. "I told you I was wrong to ignore you."

"And you said it with the sincerity of a cat walking across your laptop," I replied, stopping in the doorway to the hall. She froze in the middle of her living room, clutching the bottom hem of her shirt.

I glanced over her. She was fucking beautiful. Dark hair, blue eyes, perfectly pink, bee-stung lips. Curves everywhere you could imagine and legs for days.

But none of that mattered if she couldn't be honest about what was behind that beautiful exterior of hers.

If she couldn't break down her wall, I was done. With this conversation, and probably even the stupid experiment that led us here.

"I'm not lying to you," she said a little softer.

"Maybe you're not, but you're not telling me the whole truth. I believe that everything would have been different if I'd been able to tell you the truth about why I stood you up." I ran my fingers through my hair then shrugged. "But you don't want to talk about it, and I'm sure as fuck not going to stand here and beg you to. I'm about to enter the fight of my life thanks to Bri's maternal grandparents. I don't have the time or the inclination to fight you, too."

She straightened, defiance flashing in her eyes. "I'm not yours to fight for."

"I know that. You'll never be anyone's but your own because you're too stubborn to be honest about how you feel. You're probably not even being honest with yourself right now."

"There's no need to be fucking cruel."

"Cruel? Honesty sucks ass, Peyton, but that wasn't cruel. That was damn true, and you know it."

She bristled and pointed at me. "You don't know anything about me, Elliott. You have no idea what I'm feeling inside."

I pointed right back at her. "Because you won't let me see it! Jesus, woman. This isn't high school. I'm not going to pick you up just to tear you down because I hate the fact I ever hurt you in the first place. Remember that if it weren't for you so determined not to fall in love with someone, I wouldn't even be here right now."

"Well, I wish you weren't."

"There's something we can agree on. I'll see you around, Peyton." I waved a hand in her direction and stormed to the front door. I yanked it open, and it slammed shut behind me as I walked down the steps.

Frustration. It wound me tight. I wasn't even angry—it was just the sheer irritation at her stubbornness. At how she handled everything.

I just...I wanted to know so I could apologize for every single second I hurt her. As long as she kept those feelings wrapped up and closed off, I couldn't do that.

And more than anything, I wanted her to know it.

"Elliott!" Her voice echoed down the street behind me, but I ignored her.

I kept walking. Another block to the main road where I could grab a cab and get home.

"Elliott!" she yelled louder this time. "How would it?"

What?

"How would it what?" I finally gave in, stopping a couple houses down from hers. "What are you talking about?"

She stopped, vulnerability shadowed in her gaze. "How would it have been different?"

I said nothing.

That was one answer she wouldn't want.

"You want to be honest, so be honest with me. How would it have been different if I'd listened to you?" She stared at me, eyes wide and shining, confliction written all over her pretty face. "Well? You can't demand it of me if you won't do it yourself."

"You don't want that answer," I told her honestly.

"If I didn't want it, I wouldn't be standing in the street screaming your name and chasing you."

"You chased me for ten feet."

"That's ten feet further than I've ever chased anyone else."

The honesty in her voice struck me. It was raw— the realness I'd wanted from her.

She was right. I couldn't demand the total truth of how she felt if I wouldn't give her the truth, too.

What if this, what she wanted to know, was the final piece for her?

Would she be honest with me after?

I stuffed my hands in my pockets and rolled my shoulders. "You really wanna know what I think would have happened? If you'd stopped for thirty seconds to listen to me when I begged you to?"

She nodded. I had the feeling that, if she could run, she would.

She'd always been curious.

"If you'd let me tell you the truth about my grandmother, it would have been different. Because you'd have listened once, and even if you still hated me, you'd have come around eventually," I said.

"Is that it?"

"No. What would have really happened… I'd have fallen in love with you."

She drew in a deep breath. Her nostrils flared, and she flattened her hands against her stomach.

I knew she didn't want to hear it.

I gave her a half-hearted smile. "See you, Peyton."

She looked like she wanted to say something, but whatever it was died on her lips. She swallowed, still clutching her hands to her stomach, and dropped her eyes to the ground.

I hesitated for a few seconds before I turned and continued walking. It felt like I'd been kicked in the gut, but it was the right choice.

I was pretty sure of it.

"Stop."

It was barely there. Almost an uncertain, desperate word that'd escaped without her control.

I did it. I stopped and turned back to look at her. There was only a couple of feet between us, less than I'd thought, so she must have said it really quiet.

I watched as she closed that distance between us. She didn't speak, but I could see in her eyes that she had, for a fleeting second, let down her barrier.

Bright. Shining. Uncertain. Maybe even a little afraid.

She reached out, ghosting her fingertips across my chest. "I don't want that to be the last time you kissed me."

I opened my mouth to ask her what she meant, but she answered me before I could.

She flattened her hands against me and, sliding them to either side of my neck, Peyton went up onto her tiptoes and pressed her lips to mine.

My heart beat faster as I wrapped my arms around her body. "What do you want?" I murmured against her lips.

"To take this inside because I left my front door open."

I closed my eyes and laughed quietly at her. "All right," I said, opening my eyes. "I'll try again when we know your house isn't being robbed."

"That's great, thanks." She grinned and ran down the street to her place.

She was barefoot.

I walked into her house to find her with the freezer door open and her feet inside it. I stopped in the middle of her kitchen and frowned at the sight before me.

I had a toddler. I'd seen some weird shit, but this was right up there with the best of them.

"I might regret this," I said slowly. "But, what are you doing?"

"The ground was still a little hot," she replied, tilting her head right back so that she could look at me. "In hindsight, we should have had that whole conversation in here."

"Well..." I leaned against the fridge, crossing my arms. "That was the original plan for this."

She wrinkled up her face. "I'm sorry I was stubborn?"

"Are you asking me or telling me?"

"If I say telling, am I doing this whole adult thing right now?"

Laughter bubbled inside me. "You're doing good at not being stubborn. Given that you're sitting on the floor with your feet in the freezer, I'd hold off on proclaiming you're a good adult."

Peyton sighed heavily just as the freezer beeped. She scooted back on the floor, pulled her feet out, and pushed the door shut. "Now, my feet are cold."

"Next time you go outside, wear shoes," I offered, holding out my hands. She put her smaller ones in mine, and I pulled her up to standing. "Now, we're gonna finish that conversation."

"Right now?"

"Peyton."

She flapped her hands, jumping back from me, and make a whining kind of noise. "Okay, fine, just kill me all in one day."

"It's good to see you have a handle on that dramatic streak of yours." I smirked.

She stared at me flatly. "You're a dick, Elliott."

"And you're a drama queen, Peyton. We're going to finish this conversation even if I have to pin you down to make you talk."

"I'll scream."

"You will when we're done talking."

She opened her mouth to argue, but my meaning settled on her and tiny pink spots appeared on her cheeks. "Shut up," she said. "I knew I shouldn't have chased after you."

"Lies. All lies." I pushed off the fridge and grabbed hold of her. "You chased me because you wanted to. Now, you have to tell me what you want."

Her fingers tickled across my chest as she fidgeted. "I don't—I don't know. I want to hate you again."

"That was less complicated," I agreed.

"I want to pretend you never told me the truth, and I want to go back to thinking that you're a huge asshole who I should have beat with a hockey stick for standing me up," she continued. "But right now...I want to forget all of that." She slipped her hands up my chest and wrapped her arms around my neck. "Right now, I want you."

I raised an eyebrow, something that made her purse her lips. "Go on."

"Elliott—"

"Nope. Plying me with sex is a cop out, and you know it, woman. So, you can tell me what you're supposed to, or you can tell me what you want me to do to you." I slid my hand down over the curve of her ass and cupped it. "After all, you're not shy. I know you have a drawer full of toys upstairs."

"I do still have vintage My Little Pony figures."

"Not the toys I'm talking about."

"I know, but they're not in a drawer. They're in a locked box in my cupboard, because one time, my grandmother came around, found out, and mistook it for a bathroom decoration."

I blinked a few times as that settled in. "I have so many questions about that, but they can wait because now you're really taking the cop out."

"But, but—"

"No buts. Feelings or fucking. Make your choice before I pin you to the sofa and abstain on the fucking." As much as I didn't want to. My cock was already hardening at the thought of being inside her again.

"I want to feel you fuck me. There. I covered both bases." And judging by the grin that was spreading across her face, she was real fucking proud of herself.

"Jesus Christ, you're a sarcastic little shit."

"Don't be mean."

"Truth hurts. So does spanking."

She paused. "Not if you do it right."

"Truth or spanking?"

"Spanking. The only kind of truth I like is when my bank account tells me I can buy the fancy wine this weekend."

"I think you look good naked," I said. "Does that count as a good truth?"

Peyton raised her eyebrows. "I'm not naked right now."

"That doesn't mean I've forgotten what you look like."

"Well, then you don't need to see it again, do you?"

"All right, so I'll fuck you with my eyes closed. I'm not picky." I shrugged, and she burst out laughing.

I was bored of this.

I bent down just a little, grabbed her legs, and picked her up. She half-screamed and wriggled, but I had too tight of a grip on her for her to be able to get away.

"What are you doing, you raging Neanderthal?" she demanded as I took to the stairs.

"Me, Elliott. You, Peyton. Me, boner."

"I should have let you walk away," she said breezily, tapping her nails against my shoulder. "Should have let you go and gone to look at dick pics."

"Don't need dick pics. You can see mine for real."

"Remember when we had dinner and you told me I made you feel eighteen again? Now, I get it."

I tossed her down onto her bed. She squealed as she bounced on the mattress, and hey, maybe I threw her a little hard, but shit...

The mouth on this woman. I didn't think it could get worse than when she hated me, but holy fuck, I was wrong.

"Don't reference that again," I said, yanking my shirt over my head. "A part of me is kind of glad that we didn't get together in high school."

"We're not together now."

"I know, but I was not this good in bed back then."

She snorted. "Do I need to call Pornhub for you for auditions?"

"Why? Do you have contacts there?"

"Did you just call me a slut?"

"Did you just call me a pornstar?"

Peyton tilted her head. "I think I have a video camera somewhere. It's not impossible."

I was going to say something, then I stopped. Just looking at her, lying on her bed, hair a bit messed up, staring at me with a sparkle in her eyes...

I wasn't going to finish that sentence.

I did a Peyton and shoved that to the back of my mind.

"You took off your shirt," she said, shamelessly looking at me.

"Peyton," I said with a sigh. "My cock is hard. I'm half-naked. The only reason I'm here is because you said you wanted to have sex with me."

She dropped her head back, laughing. "You make it sound like I found out you're a Russian spy, and I'm blackmailing you!"

I froze. "Shit. You know about that?"

"I went through your underwear drawer when you weren't looking. I found the papers," she said solemnly. "Multiple me again, and I won't turn you in."

"Now, that's blackmail."

She nodded. "I take my orgasms very seriously."

"Unlike your feet." I laughed quietly and headed over to her. She sat up, and in seconds, I put to bed any further conversation.

I took her soft lips with mine, kissing her slowly. She kept one hand on the bed to prop her up, but the other ran through my hair in a way that sent a shiver through my body.

It was crazy how much she affected me.

My cock pushed against the zipper of my jeans, and all that did was remind me of how badly I wanted her. I pulled back to remove her shirt. She reached for me, pulling me down to lie with her.

Peyton ran her hands up and down my arms as we kissed. Goosebumps popped up in the wake of her touch, but I didn't care. I didn't care if she knew how bad I wanted her right now or how crazy she was making me.

I stroked her thighs until my fingers found their way to her waistband. She didn't object to me pulling down her denim shorts and tossing them aside, leaving her in her underwear.

Her skin flushed as I moved my mouth downward, over the curve of her neck and the swell of her tits. I unhooked her bra, almost failing, and cupped both of her tits with my hands.

Rough palming and hot kisses had her breathing heavy and her back arching. I kept my hands where they were as I moved further down. I dropped kisses all down her stomach until I reached the band of her satin thong.

She trembled, her stomach visibly tightening when I ran a finger along there.

I took the thong off, too.

Me in my jeans and her completely naked, I dropped to my knees and parted her legs. She had her hands at the bottom of her stomach, and I saw her shaking as I kissed the inside of her thigh.

She threw one arm up to cover her eyes the second my mouth brushed over her pussy. I stopped her from closing her legs by gripping her thighs and keeping them open.

My blood pumped hot as I ran my tongue over my pussy. Knowing that I'd barely touched her here and she was already losing control turned me on more.

Knowing I affected her the way she did me?

I went in hard. Just to prove it. To show *her* that she wanted me more than she wanted to admit.

I explored her pussy with my tongue. Teasing and toying with her clit made her moan and writhe, and it didn't take long before she gripped the quilt and her knuckles went white.

I kept my eyes on her as I licked her. It didn't matter that hers were covered. I could see the flush of red as it grew up her neck to her cheeks. I could see how her lips parted with each uncontrollable moan, how her chest heaved as she struggled to even her breathing.

I could see how I affected her, how close she was to the edge, and I was about to take her there.

I tilted my head and, with pressure on her clit from my flattened tongue, rubbed it. Over and over, unrelentingly, I circled it until Peyton's body clammed up, her thighs squeezing my head, and she moaned out an "Oh my God, oh my God," followed by something incoherent.

I kissed her pussy, then her thigh, and parted her legs so I could stand. She was gasping, totally wiped, and I undid my jeans.

That got her attention.

She dropped her arm and looked up. Looked down, to be more precise. My cock was bulging out of my boxers, and I wanted it fucking out.

I opened the top drawer of her nightstand and pulled a condom from the box.

"Aw, you remember where I keep them," she said with a laugh.

I tore open the packet and dropped the wrapper on the floor. "I listen, and I remember the important things."

"I appreciate your thoughtfulness."

"Peyton? Shut up."

"Elliott? Make me." Her eyes danced with desire and laughter.

I rolled the condom on over my cock and covered her body with mine. It'd be my pleasure to shut her up, only to make her scream soon enough.

"You taste like me," she murmured against my lips, reaching down between our bodies and wrapping her fingers around my cock.

She stilled.

"What?" I asked, pulling my face back from hers enough to meet her eyes.

Her forehead twitched into a bit of a frown. "Will your mom mind that you're still here and she has Briony?"

"Peyton. This is not a conversation I want to have when your hand is wrapped around my cock."

"Right. Sorry. Never mind."

"Quick. Before this moment is lost forever," I demanded. "Seriously, shut up and let me fuck you. Not another damn word unless you're praying to me."

"The ego…" She rolled her eyes, but she did as she'd been told, raising her hips and guiding me into her.

If she was any less hot and I was any less frustrated, there was no way she'd be this lucky that I was still hard.

I tossed the unhelpful interruption from my mind and kissed her. She was hot and wet around me, and she squeezed my cock tight.

Just like that, everything else disappeared.

There was only Peyton, beneath me, gasping and moaning with her nails in my back. There was only how she felt, how she reacted, how her legs twitched, and her breathing hitched.

There was me, inside her. Her legs tight around my waist. Gripping me. Holding me in place as if I'd move before she was done—before we both were.

There was the innate satisfaction of her tight pussy hugging my cock as I thrust back and forth. Of my fingers in her hair as I kissed her, so her moans disappeared into my mouth.

There was just her.

Her. An orgasm. The trembling of her legs and the moaning from her mouth. The almost painful grip of her nails as they sliced into my shoulders.

The red-hot rush of pleasure as I came, too.

I buried myself inside her, my grip on her tight as I gave in.

Even when I was done, I didn't let go.

And neither did she.

CHAPTER FOURTEEN

PEYTON

Talking after sex is overrated. What are you supposed to say? "Thanks for the bang, buh-bye now! Don't forget to take your number with you!"

ELLIOTT WALKED OUT OF THE BATHROOM WITH HIS boxers back on. "I'm amazed that I just saw you crawl to the bathroom to pee."

"I take my sexual health seriously," I said, looking up from hooking my bra back into place. "That, and I couldn't walk."

"I did notice you were like a newborn Bambi." He stopped in the middle of the room. "Why do you pee after sex? They don't show that in the movies."

"I doubt peeing in toilets is sexy in porn."

"Normal movies, woman. Normal movies."

"Ohhh." I slapped my forehead, although I knew what he meant. "Well, in that case, there are a lot of movie stars with fake infections."

"Peeing stops STDs?"

"Maybe in porn," I said. "UTI's. They hurt like a bitch."

Elliott tilted his head to the side. "Huh. How does that help? Is it female voodoo?"

I stared at him wearily. "I'm still recovering. Can we not talk about pee right after sex?"

"You brought up my mother right in the middle of it."

"Out of concern!" I threw my arms in the air. "It hit me that she knows you came to talk to me!"

He laughed and sat on the bed with you. "Peyton, I am a twenty-seven-year-old adult male on my way to talk to a very attractive adult woman. I think my mother would have been more surprised if I were home already, but I can text her if you'd feel better."

"I'm not, I mean, Briony was sick."

"Briony ate three pieces of cheesecake for dinner because my mother is weak," he retorted, getting up and retrieving his phone from his pants. "If she's still sick, Mom gets the cleanup duty this time."

"That was the first thing she ate? Everyone knows you give toast."

He looked at me with a sympathetic smile. "Ah. You're unaware of the toddler handbook. If they can keep down a slice of toast, that means they get two bananas, a yoghurt, a handful of candy, three juice boxes, and three slices of cheesecake."

That was a lot of food.

"Wow. And I thought the fact I could eat six tacos on Tuesdays was impressive."

He pointed his phone at me. "Still impressive. But toddlers have everyone beat. Except for teenage boys."

That was true. My parents went from one grocery shop a week to three by the time my brother had turned thirteen.

No wonder he had to pay rent when he got a job and I didn't...

"There we go," Elliott said. "See? It's fine." He tossed the phone my way, then picked his pants back up again.

"You don't have to do anything drastic like wear pants," I said, peering over at him. "I'm an advocate of the no-pants life."

"I'm an advocate of the naked life if you're keeping score."

I rolled my eyes and looked at the phone.

Elliott: All ok? Will be back soon.

Mom: B's asleep and your dad is on his fishing trip. I'm fine here. You stay and have all the sex.

"That is not normal for a mom to say," I said, handing it back.

"Your grandmother mistook a dildo for bathroom décor."

He had a point...

"Which you're going to explain to me right now."

"Ugh, fine. But I need water. And ice-cream, probably," I said, getting up. I grabbed a tank top from the drawer and a clean pair of panties. I threw both items on quickly and followed Elliott down to my kitchen.

To where a very familiar male was rifling through my kitchen drawers.

"Dominic!" I shouted. "What are you doing?" I hid behind Elliott.

"Peyt, seriously?" Elliott wriggled out of my grasp. "I'm as naked as you are!"

Dom jumped, almost hitting his head on the open cupboard door.

Damn it. If it were me, I'd have hit it.

"What are you doing?" I shouted again.

My brother looked at me. "Why are you half-naked?"

I tugged my shirt down as far as possible, almost choking on laughter when I saw Elliott side-shuffle to the living room and grab a cushion to cover his groin with.

"It's my house, and if I want to walk around half-naked, I can do that," I snapped.

"Why's he half-naked?" He nodded toward Elliott.

"Because we were practicing line dancing," I snapped. "Why do you think?"

Dom frowned. "I thought you were supposed to be sleeping with Elliott Sloane."

I held an arm out in Elliott's direction and waved it in frustration. "Elliott Sloane!"

Recognition dawned on Dom's face. "Oh, well, shit. Good to see you, Elliott."

"I never thought I'd have to say this," Elliott said. "But can you turn around, so I can get pants on for this cozy reunion?"

Dom immediately turned around.

"You want some?" Elliott asked me.

"No. If he breaks into my house, it's not my fault if he sees me without pants. He's lucky he didn't break in twenty minutes ago," I replied, walking across to the fridge. I pulled out a bottle of water.

"Fair enough." Elliott walked over to the stairs.

You could kind of see the stairs from where I was standing, so I leaned over and watched as he went up.

Seriously.

That ass could make lesbians cry. It was peachier than the state of Georgia.

"What are you doing?" Dom asked.

I snapped my head around to him. "Are you eating my food?"

He shrugged, tearing a bite off the pizza slice.

"That pizza is two days old."

He coughed and spat it out into his hand, then dumped it into my trashcan.

I hid my smile by sipping my water. It wasn't. It was, like, two or three hours old, but the revenge was fun.

"You're gross," he said. "What is he doing here?"

"Watering my lady garden," I replied. "What the hell are you doing here?"

"Looking for documents." He shoved his hands in his pockets. "I'm finalizing our expenses, but I think Chloe gave them to you for safekeeping."

Seriously. We couldn't trust him with a key, but he was trusted to do taxes. That was testament to how much Chloe hated numbers.

Me? I shoved it all in a folder through the year and paid someone to do it for me.

Clearly, I was the Austin sibling with the brains.

"I do have your expenses, but why you need them right now, I don't know." I pulled out a chair and sat down.

"Chloe said you had no appointments until one tomorrow, so you were coming in late. I want to do it in the morning."

"Have you heard of this new thing? It's really cool. It has an eight-inch screen and has this really cool function where you can talk to people without breaking into their houses," I said dryly.

Dom flipped me the bird. "I called, and you didn't answer."

"I was busy."

"I know that now."

"Be patient next time. And don't break in."

"It wasn't breaking in. The door was unlocked."

I put my bottle down and stared at him. "You didn't touch my keys, did you?"

"Funny. Can I have the expenses? I'm weirded the fuck out having this conversation with you wearing nothing."

I crossed one leg over the other and leaned back in my seat. "Then, don't break into my house."

"The door was open!" he yelled.

"Send a text message!" I shouted right back.

Seriously. I'd had a day of shit. The only good thing had been the sex, and even now that was ruined.

"Give me the expenses, and I'll leave you alone," he said.

I shook my head. "Chloe told me that, under absolutely no circumstances barring a coma or death, am I to give you the expenses."

Dom threw his arms up in the air and leaned against my counter. "This is bullshit. I need the expenses to do the tax."

"You lose everything, man!" I was trying not to laugh now, but it really was quite ridiculous.

Unfortunately for my brother, I'd seen my sweet friend when she got mad, and you know how they say not to feed the Gremlins?

That. Don't feed Chloe.

"C'mon, Peyt."

"No. I'm not giving you the file. She'll kill me if you lose all the physical ones because you can't get those back. I'll text her, and she can get them in the morning for you."

Elliott came back down and tossed me a pair of yoga pants. "Here."

I put them on the table and had another drink of water. While a now fully-clothed Elliott and my asshole brother reunited, I slid my phone across the table and dialed Chloe.

"What?" she wheezed.

"What are you doing?"

"Yoga."

"Stop for a minute."

"I can't. Hold on. Downward Dog time."

"Chloe! My brother is here and almost interrupted me having sex."

There was a crash on the end of her line just as Dom yelled: "No, I didn't!"

"Sorry. I fell over," she said, coming back on the line. "Dom did what?"

"Nothing!" Dom yelled, trying to get my phone. "Nothing!"

I put the water down, smacked away Dom's hand, and put it on speaker. "He said he's come for the expenses."

"Don't you dare give them to him!" Chloe shouted down the line. "I will hunt you down and cut you, Peyton. Do not give the king of losing things something that important."

Elliott smirked from the other side of the kitchen, his arms folded over his chest.

"See, Dom? I told you. I can't give you the receipts."

"Shit! Am I on speaker?"

"Yes," I told Chloe. "You are."

"Uh, who's there? You said something about sex. Is that with a person or…?"

"Chloe," I deadpanned.

"Is it Elliott? Or someone else?"

Did I have a reputation I wasn't fully aware of?

"Elliott. All I want is for you to tell Dom that he's Losey McLoserson and he can't have the expenses."

"Oh, this is awkward. Hi, Elliott."

"Hi, Chloe," he called over the room.

Dom clapped his hands. "The fucking expenses, Chlo! I need them."

There was a crackle that sounded like her sighing. "Nope. I'll come by Peyton's tomorrow on my way into the office and get them. It's not like you can get in there without me, anyway."

Elliott covered his mouth with his hand.

"Fine. Then, I'm not leaving here unless I have the expenses," Dom said.

What? No. No, fuck off. That was not how this shit worked, Dominic.

"Excuse me?" I blinked at him several times. "You're leaving."

"Not without my expenses."

"Dominic, you're thirty. Stop being childish," Chloe chided him through the phone. "Leave her alone. She's busy."

"She already got laid. She's fine."

I got up and grabbed my water. "Someone bring me my phone when y'all are done. I'm fed up of this already." I threw a wave over my shoulder and headed upstairs.

"Put on some pants!" Dom shouted after me.

"Get some responsibility!" I yelled back when I reached the top of my stairs. I went to my room and slammed the door behind me.

Goddamn it. Not only was Dom all in my business, now, I knew I'd have a million questions.

About something I wasn't entirely sure if I cared about anymore.

I knew it was possible to have sex with someone three times and not fall in love with them.

I just didn't know if I could do that with Elliott— not without taking a huge risk.

My door opened, and Elliott slipped inside. "Hey," he said, shutting it behind him. "Are you okay?"

"He's like herpes," I replied. "And crabs. And chicken pox, all put together in one frustrating illness."

"That sounds like it might kill someone." He laughed lightly and sat on the bed next to me. "I tried to convince him to leave."

"I take it that didn't go well."

Elliott shook his head, sighed, and leaned back. He propped himself up on his elbows, and I shifted to look at him. "In fact, I think I made it worse."

"Oh, God," I moaned, leaning back against the headrest of the bed. "What did you do?"

"I told him it'd taken me two orgasms to get you out of a bad mood, and I didn't appreciate him putting you back in that shitty one."

"That doesn't seem so bad."

"Then, he asked me why I cared so much, and I asked him why he was hell-bent on pissing off the women in his life."

"So, the reunion went well," I said sarcastically.

He shrugged a shoulder. "He's the reason all this is happening. I don't need him to like me."

"Nobody needs my brother to like them. It's more of a headache than it's worth." I pushed my hair behind my ear. "Are you going home?"

"Why would I go home? Did you hear Chloe on the phone? If Dom is staying, I'm going to be here when shit goes down."

I stared at him. He looked like an excited kid the way his eyes sparkled at the prospect.

I held up my hands. "Fine, but I'm not going anywhere near him. And for the love of God, please bring me my keys."

Elliott got up and stopped at the door. "What's with the key thing?"

"He loses everything. He's lost so many keys to his side of the office that Chloe has to have the locks changed."

"For one key?"

"No. At least four in the last year."

"How does anyone lose that many keys?"

I shrugged. "Ask him. We haven't figured it out yet."

***

The shrill ring of my phone broke through the semi-conscious, sleepy haze I was in where I was neither awake or asleep.

Reaching my arm out toward the nightstand, I felt around for it, groaning when I knocked it off onto the floor. My head was heavy, and my eyes were still sticky with sleep, but I managed to retrieve the phone from next to the bed and answer it.

"Hello?" I groaned.

"Peyton?" Chloe's voice sounded in my ear.

"Why are you calling me so early?"

"It's seven-thirty. Hardly early. You need to let me in, so I can get the expenses and remove the wart from your living room."

That was music to my half-asleep ears.

"Give me a minute." I hung up, yawned, and forced myself to sit up.

At least, I tried to.

There was something around my waist. Something that, when I looked, I discovered to be a tanned, muscled arm. Following the arm, my gaze led me to the face of Elliott Sloane.

Right. I forgot he was still here.

I dumped his arm off me—if I was awake, he could be awake, too—and got out of bed. I quickly got dressed and, retrieving my keys from the floor, went down to let Chloe in.

"You look like crap," she said, strolling past me into the hall.

"Good morning, sunshine," I replied, pushing the door shut behind her and following her into the room.

Right at that moment, Dom walked into the kitchen, waist wrapped in a bright purple towel. Chloe stopped dead, blushing.

"What are you doing?" I demanded. "Why are you here? Why are you using my shower?"

He pulled a mug from the cupboard and grabbed a coffee pod. "I'm making a coffee. I'm here for expenses. And I needed a shower. By the way, you need a more comfortable sofa for your guests to sleep on."

"I have a two-bedroom house where one is an office for a reason. I don't want guests. Especially not if you're it." I snatched the mug from him and made the coffee for myself.

"Dom." Chloe sighed, putting her purse on the table. "You're thirty this year. Do you have to be such an insufferable fuckhead all the time?"

"I have taxes to do," he replied. "Which I can't do without expenses."

"You lose everything like a five-year-old. No, a five-year-old is more responsible than you are," she shot back without missing a beat. "You lose your keys, your phone is misplaced twice a day, and you lost my coffee mug because you used it when yours went missing... In Peyton's office."

"I didn't lose your mug." He gripped the towel, refusing to look at her.

"Well, I didn't lose it. Or your phone. Or your keys."

Elliott slipped in next to me. "Did I miss it?"

"Shh," I said, reaching behind me for the latte I'd just made.

He nodded, leaning back against the counter next to me and folding his arms as we watched them fight.

"I don't lose my phone. I just forget where I put it sometimes." Dom clutched tighter at his towel. "I wouldn't lose the expenses."

"Where have I heard that before?" She folded one arm over her chest and tapped a finger against her lips. "Oh, yeah, the last two times I handed you new office keys. Which, by the way, I found your keyring in my car this morning. So, not only are you too incompetent to keep hold of them, you lose them in different places."

"You found my keyring? Are you finding my keys and withholding them?"

"No. I don't want to be your babysitter in and out of the building you live in, you turd. I want you to grow a pair and not lose your keys every ten seconds!"

"Then, cut me a new key."

"So you can lose it again?"

"You won't be my babysitter anymore, Chlo."

"No." She jabbed her finger at him. "Until you can keep the key to your apartment for one whole month without losing it, you do not have the office key."

Dom let go of the towel, only to have to snatch it back when it almost fell down.

Elliott took my cup of coffee and finished it. Usually, that was a mortal sin that came with a sentence of certain death, but the domestic between my best friend and brother was way more entertaining.

"You can't lock me out of my office!" Dom shouted.

"I don't need to! You lock yourself out when you lose your keys!"

We were this close to a screaming match.

"Should we leave?" Elliott leaned in to mutter.

I shook my head. "I have a feeling we haven't hit the jackpot yet."

Dom adjusted the towel once more. Put some freaking pants on, bro. "I don't know how I work with you."

Fury lit up Chloe's eyes. "I don't know how I work with you! You're disorganized and intolerable. Not to mention you haven't grasped that there's only one thing you're supposed to lose and never find again: your virginity!"

CHAPTER FIFTEEN

PEYTON

There was more than one way to get burned.
Fire. Ice. Sunshine.
Women before coffee.

I SUCKED IN A BREATH.

"Burn," Elliott whispered to me.

Dom stared at her for a minute before turning and storming off without a word. Chloe glared after him until Elliott cleared his throat.

"Do you want a coffee?" he offered.

Chloe jerked around, as if she'd forgotten where she was. "Oh, um, thanks, but I should probably grab those expenses and leave. And lock him out."

I snorted. "You know where they are in my office."

She smiled, cheeks flushed, and ducked her head as she ran to my stairs.

"Is it just me," Elliott started when I turned to put my cup under the coffee machine again, "Or is there something between them?"

I nodded, changing out the pod. "For years. I'm waiting for the moment it finally implodes."

"And another thing!" Dom yelled, storming into the front room.

Plus pants.

Thank God.

"She's upstairs," I said, pushing the button.

"Shit," he muttered. "That was a good comeback, too."

"You know the only comeback you should give her? Kiss her," I told him, turning around. "Y'all's foreplay is longer than a teenage virgin's."

"I don't have a thing for her," he lied, his face expressionless. "She drives me crazy."

"You have a thing for her," Elliott said.

Dom raised his eyebrows. "Like you have a thing for my sister?"

Elliott shrugged. "I'm sleeping with her, aren't I?"

"You have a thing for me?" I said, looking at him.

"I didn't wake up with a boner over French toast, Peyton."

Well. There it was. The confirmation my brother needed to grill my ass all day long.

I was going to kill Elliott.

"Got it," Chloe said, walking back into the room. "Thanks."

Dom glared at her.

"Don't look at me like that," she said. "I'm not going to change my mind."

"Fine. File your own taxes," he shot back. "You've never done that in your life."

"Who do you think did my taxes before we went into business together? Which, by the way, second biggest mistake of my life!" Chloe clutched the folder to her chest.

"What's the first?" Elliott whispered.

I shrugged. "Maybe dating Rory Wilson in eighth grade?"

"Your dad did your taxes!" Dom replied. "And by God, if you think this is the second biggest mistake of your life and feel anything like I do about it, then your first one must be one hell of a fuck-up!"

Chloe stared at him, unmoving. Was she even breathing? Her silence was chilling, and Elliott actually took a step closer to me.

"Oh, it is," she said, her cold tone slicing through the air. "It was when I had a crush on you. Once upon a time."

On that, she left.

My brother stared after her, dumbfounded, unable to move.

I stared at the door.

Had I just watched my best friend's heart break?

"Well," Elliott said, breaking the silence. "That was a plot twist."

Maybe if you weren't privy to the fact she was helplessly in love with him, and that was why she got so mad at him. I didn't get it, but it was how she coped with keeping those feelings cooped up inside.

"She used to have a crush on me?" Dom asked, turning his head to look at me. "Did you know that?"

"Of course!" I snapped, pushing off the counter. "You just have the eyesight of a bat and the understanding of a saber-tooth tiger."

"The tigers are dead."

"Exactly!" I walked over to him and smacked his arm. "Jesus, Dom. How do you two not kill each other?"

"Skill and a weekly agreement over who buys breakfast. If I kill her, she won't bring me anything to eat."

I shook my head. "If I were you, don't go to work today. Shit, I can't believe I'm saying this—stay here. I have to go and check on her, so stay here, and I'll bring your computer back here."

"Does that mean you'll give me a key?"

I pursed my lips. "The only key you need is the one to access a florist website to buy Chloe some flowers. And me, while you're at it."

"You? Why do you need flowers?"

"You hurt my friend, and you pissed me off by breaking in."

"I didn't break in."

"Dominic Nathaniel Austin," I snapped.

Good Lord, I sounded like my mother.

"Is Mom here? Is she stuffed in a closet somewhere?" he asked.

I turned around, ready to punch him again. Unfortunately, Elliott darted between us and held me back, but that didn't stop me yelling at him. "None of this would have happened if you weren't such a fucking tool last night!" I swung my arm to point at him and almost hit Elliott.

He let me go with a murmured apology to my brother.

Dom's eyes widened.

"You are thirty in two months! Thirty!" More finger jabbing in his direction. "You are a hot mess of a man who can't be trusted with the expenses of his own business, and instead of accepting your shortcomings, you refused to leave when I wouldn't give you the documents. This entire situation is because of your stubborn, pig-headedness, and no. Don't you dare open your mouth to argue with me."

He closed it.

Maybe he had more brains than I thought.

"You know it's true. You acted like a fucking child who couldn't find the cookie jar, and congratulations, you got into yet another screaming fight with Chloe. Except this time, you hurt her. Which means you hurt me, because I'm the one who has to go and see her cry out yet another frustration over your stupidly obstinate ways!"

For the first time in my life, I saw him look ashamed.

"She is worth ten of you on her worst day, Dom, and you're not even a bad person. You're a disaster sometimes, but you're my brother, and I love you. And that's why I'm telling you this. You need a reality check. I just had one, so it's time you did, too."

"Someone gave you a reality check?" He raised his eyebrows. "Did they chain you to a wall?"

Before I had the chance to say a word, Elliott stepped in front of me. He pushed me behind him, closing down any chance of me arguing back at him.

"No. She decided that high school was ten years ago, and she wasn't a fucktard teen anymore." His voice was so low with a cold edge that I bristled. "She listened, and she thought, and she was big enough to accept what she did wrong. You should try it, Dom. You might find yourself enlightened."

Dom stepped to the side and met my eyes. "Does he speak for you, now? Did you decide to fall in love instead of just screwing him?"

I shoved Elliott to the side and stared at my brother. "I'm going to get changed. If I see you here on my way out, I'm going to drag you out by your measly penis."

"Terrified."

"And then I'll call Mimi." That was my parting shot as I headed up the stairs to my room to get changed.

Something—some*one*—was under my brother's skin, but that didn't mean I'd take his asshole ways.

He acted more like a teenager than he did when he was a teen.

***

Luckily for Dom, he hadn't been anywhere to be found when I left. Neither had Elliott, but I wasn't surprised by that. He'd come up to tell me his mom had a lunchtime appointment at the salon, so he had to get back for Briony, and I agreed to call him when I was done with Chloe.

I hoped he didn't expect me anytime soon. I couldn't find her, even though the main door was open. The door that leads to the stairs to Dom's apartment was locked, so I tried the Stupid Cupid office.

Open.

"Chlo?" I gently called, walking into their spacious office. Given that there were two of them, I'd happily given up the bigger space, and they had a pull-out wall installed between their desks.

Both were empty, and so was the bathroom that was connected to Dom's side of the room.

I tried my office.

Unlocked.

Only two other people had the key to my office.

Mellie.

And Chloe.

I slowly opened the door. She was sitting on my sofa, legs curled beneath her. The expenses folder was on the armchair with her purse, and she cradled a coffee mug as if it grounded her.

"Chlo," I repeated, this time much softer than before.

She looked up, her thick, mascara-coated lashes peering at me through a thin curtain of her blond hair. "I quit," she said quietly. "I'm going to work with you instead."

Despite her sadness, I laughed. "No, you're not. You couldn't take all the cocks."

"Words every pornstar heard," she muttered.

"Hey, if you wanna be the next Lisa Ann, I'm all about that life." I sat on the sofa next to her and stroked her hair. "He's a dick."

"I don't care," she said nonchalantly.

"Yes, you do. Otherwise, you'd have stabbed him in the crotch and told the cops that he deserved it."

She sniffed, looking at the mug I now realized was empty.

I took it from her.

"Chlo...Why do you do this to yourself? He's an immature prick. He's not good enough for you."

She looked up at me. "How can you say that? He's your brother."

"Because blood doesn't trump character. He's a dick. He needs a slap upside the head with a shovel. You're my best friend, and I'm telling you right now, unless he does a one-eighty to apologize, I want to drag you away until you get over him."

"I don't—"

"Don't. I know you're in love with him. You've been in love with him since at least second grade when you slapped him with your spade because he kicked over your sandcastle."

She snort-laughed. "I thought we'd never be friends after that."

"Eh. I'd have done it for you," I told her. "Seriously, Chlo, he's not worth you. He's a child in a man's body. And for what it's worth, he was shaken as shit that you told him you used to have a crush on him."

"Oh my God." She buried her face in her hands. "Why did I say that? Peyton. Why didn't you stop me?"

"Because," I said gently. "Maybe you needed to say it. You needed to burst it out of your system, so you could look at the conversation for what it was."

"I don't know." She dropped her hands and looked up at me. "It's never going to happen, is it? Me and him. He's so dumb. I can't believe he's made it almost thirty years without killing himself."

"Well, there was that time in second grade where he thought it would be a good idea to spray deodorant into Mimi's open fire."

"That's why it's so amazing," she muttered. "What's even more impressive is that I haven't killed him yet. Or you, for that matter."

She had a point.

"See? Miracles do exist. He's like a cat."

"Yeah, well, he's probably used eight of those lives already," Chloe said. She pulled out two silver keys. "These are his keys."

My lips twitched. "You have his keys?"

She nodded. "One was stuffed down the back of the couch, and the other was in a bottle of Tylenol."

I did a double-take. "Inside the bottle? How did it get inside the bottle?"

She tossed them onto the coffee table and held up her hands. "I don't know how it's remotely possible."

There was one to ask later.

"You know you told him you don't have his keys," I said. "But those seem like stupid places to put keys."

"Yeah, well, he's stupid."

Well, she wasn't wrong there. I could have told her that.

But still, who lost a key in a—

"Chloe," I said slowly.

"What?"

"He's messing with you."

She stared at me, jaw dropping.

"The sofa cushions? Fine. I've probably got ten bucks in quarters down the back of this thing." I tapped my sofa. "But in a Tylenol bottle?"

"I did think it was—" she stopped, gasping. She smacked her hands over her mouth. "I told him last week I needed Tylenol for a headache and he told me there was some in the bathroom cupboard!"

My eyes widened. "Was the bottle it was in empty?"

She shook her head, hands still in front of her mouth. "Oh my God. He knows I lied."

I wanted to be more shocked about that, but... "You both lied. He hid them, you found them. You should put them back to annoy him."

She snorted and stood up. She swiped the keys in one quick movement, then stormed to my door. "And let him get back in the office without me? No way. Inconveniencing him is better revenge."

"Okay," I said, rolling my head around to look at her. "If you think he didn't make copies before he did that, you're an idiot."

"Oh, no, I know he made copies." An evil grin spread across her face. "But he doesn't know I know."

"And as long as you have the "lost" keys he has to keep this shit up," I finished.

She pointed the keys at me, grin still firmly in place as she backed out of my space. "Exactly."

I stared at the blank doorway for a minute, then came the sound of her laughter from across the hall.

Man. Those two were fucked up.

***

"I like ponies. Do you like ponies?" Briony looked up from where she was playing with what was apparently My Little Pony toys and a castle.

I didn't remember any of these ponies.

"I like ponies," I answered.

"I like pincesses. Do you like pincesses?"

"Sure. I like princesses."

"Who's your fadorit?"

Three-year-olds. They had a whole other language, didn't they?

"I don't know…" I trailed off at the sight of Elliott in the doorway. His lips were moving, but I didn't know what he was saying.

"Cinderella," he mouthed. "Cinderella."

Ohhh.

"Peydon? Who's your fadorit pincess?" Briony waved at me to get my attention.

I pretended to really think hard about it. "I don't know. That's really tough."

She closed her eyes and with all the wisdom of girl who knew the struggles of choosing a princess, nodded solemnly.

"I think I have to pick Cinderella, though."

She gasped. Her eyes flew open, and she dropped the pony she was holding to smack her hands against her cheeks in delight. "I lub her, too! She's my fadorit! Daddy! Daddy!" She scrambled up off the floor and ran to Elliott.

I leaned back to see her go.

"Daddy." She tugged on his shirt. "Daddy. Daddy, where ared you?"

"In the bathroom," Elliott said, sounding a little reluctant. "What is it?"

There were heavy footsteps as Briony charged to the downstairs toilet and leaned against the door. "Daddy! Daddy. Daddy. Comed here."

"I'm busy right now, baby."

"Den open the door so I can telled you."

"I'd really prefer not to."

"Daddy! Daddy!" She knocked on the door. "I need to telled you something!"

"I can hear you just fine," he said wearily. "Go ahead and tell me."

I covered my mouth with my hand so my laughter wouldn't get out.

"But I don't wanna talked to the door. I wanna talked to you," Briony argued.

"Briony, I'm on the toilet. Be patient." His voice was a little firmer now.

"But—"

"No. Wait for a second."

Her lower lip wobbled, and she dipped her head to look at the floor. She didn't move, she simply stood there silently, her face hidden by a curtain of her hair that was, today, poofed from being in a braid all day.

I stayed sitting awkwardly on the sofa. This was definitely a parenting thing—one I had no experience with. This was only the second time I'd ever met her, after all.

After a good minute of silence, the bathroom door opened, and I watched as Elliott wiped his hands on his pants, leaving wet marks on them, and crouched down to Briony's level.

Gently, he put two fingers under her chin and lifted her head. "We spoke about being patient, didn't we? Especially when someone is using the toilet."

She nodded.

"Especially when we have guests. I can't leave the door unlocked, okay? I'm sure Peyton doesn't want to see me poop."

And that was way too much information for today.

Briony turned her head and looked at me. Ignoring Elliott's amused smile, I shook my head in agreement that I most definitely did not want to witness him pooping.

"I sorry," Briony said.

"That's okay. You'll remember next time." He kissed her forehead.

He had more faith than I did.

"Now, what did you want to tell me?"

She immediately brightened. "Oh, Daddy, Daddy! Peydon likes Cinderella, too!"

Elliott put on one of the most convincing shocked-faced I'd ever seen. "No. Really?"

"Uh-huh, uh-huh." She nodded her head frantically. "Can we watched it?"

Wait…

"The first one or the butterfly one?"

"Budderfly."

The butterfly one? "What's the butterfly one?" I asked.

"The live-action one," Elliott answered, scooping Briony up. He set her on his hip and carried her over to where I was on the sofa. "There are butterflies on the blue dress."

"Huh. I've never seen it."

Elliott's eyebrows shot up.

Briony gasped, grabbing hold of my arms with her tiny, chubby hands. "You never seed it? Daddy, Peydon has to watched it immediwatly!"

"Okay, okay, calm down." He was laughing. "Maybe Peyton can't stay long enough to watch the movie. Did you think of that?"

"No," she said bluntly. "She didn't seed it, so she has to stay."

"She might not be able to stay over dinner."

"Den she won't get to see it."

Three-year-old logic.

Terrifyingly flawless.

"Why don't you ask her?" Elliott said. "I'm sure that's much better than demanding, isn't it?"

She sighed and looked up at me. She even leaned into me, practically climbing on my lap to ask—

Never mind. She was on my lap. And the girl's knees were so sharp she could slice stone.

Briony touched two hands to my face. They were warm against my cheeks, and she held me firm as she looked into my eyes. "Peydon."

She looked so serious with her little blue eyes and ribbon lips that I had to really try to not laugh at her.

"Briony," I repeated.

"Can you stay to watched Cinderella? I will made you an apple juice from the fridge if you can."

How the hell did I say no to that?

Answer: I didn't.

CHAPTER SIXTEEN

ELLIOTT

Toddlers are persistent.
A bit like hemorrhoids.

"THAT SOUNDS FUN," PEYTON SAID. "AND APPLE JUICE? I love apple juice!"

I didn't have to see Bri's face to know she was beaming with delight. Apple juice and Cinderella were her two true loves in this world, so to have found someone else who felt the same way?

Shoot her down—she was in love with Peyton based on that alone.

"Okay!" Bri turned around. "Daddy, you get the moodie, and I'll get the apple juice."

She scrambled down off of Peyton's lap and ran into the kitchen.

"Is she okay with that juice?" Peyton watched her go.

I selected the Blu-ray from the cupboard and shot a smirk her way. "Sorry to break it to you, but you're getting a juice box."

"I can live with that."

I turned away and hit the eject button on the player. "You didn't have to say yes to her, you know."

"Of course, I had to. Have you seen those eyes? How do you say no to her, ever?"

"I think of all the times she screams and swings her arms like a tiny terrorist, and it's pretty easy." I put the disk in and turned around.

Peyton had one eyebrow raised. "See, now, I'd think that's reason to say no."

"It depends on the day. Sometimes it results in her being put to bed to calm down, which means she ends up taking a rare afternoon nap, and I get some peace and quiet."

"That's a thing around her? She was talking to me for thirty minutes flat about what I did and didn't like."

"Only thirty minutes? Lucky you. She has about three hours of material of that." I took a seat on the sofa, making sure to leave space between us for Bri. "Did she get started on hedgehogs yet?"

Peyton looked a little confused. "Hedgehogs?"

"YouTube is the devil."

"That…was quite the jump in subject."

I laughed as the main menu music hit on the TV. "I'm going to preface this by saying kids are weird."

"Some get that from their parents."

I blinked at her for a second. She wasn't wrong if half these people who had a mini-career opening fucking toys on YouTube were parents.

"There are a bunch of stupid videos on YouTube, and apparently, watching people open toys is thrilling."

Now, she looked really confused.

"And on one of those she watched, the person had a pet hedgehog who wasn't having the nonsense of her opening a Hatchimal on camera, so it stole the egg."

She blinked several times in quick succession. "I have no idea what you just said, and if I'm honest… Please don't explain it."

I laughed and hit play on the TV.

"Here's your dooce-box," Briony said, handing Peyton two. "And das mine. I can't do the straws."

"Oh. Right. Okay." Peyton looked at the two juices that had been thrust at her.

Smiling, I took one from her. I pulled the straw off the back, out of the tiny plastic slip, and poked it through the foiled hole in the top. "There you go," I said to Briony. "What do you want for dinner?"

She put the straw in her mouth and pursed her lips as she sucked the juice up. Peyton watched her, lips twitching, as she put her straw in place.

"Pizza!" Briony announced.

Oh no. I'd eaten too much pizza lately.

Was there such a thing as too much pizza?

Maybe if the toppings were changed up...

"Peydon, do you want pizza?" Bri asked, leaning right into her.

"I like pizza," she replied, smiling sweetly down at her. "What's your favorite?"

"I like spots and cheese."

"Spots?"

I coughed on my water. "Pepperoni," I explained. "They look like spots on the pizza."

Peyton's eyes met mine for a minute. Silent laughter shone back at me. That really was toddler logic at its finest.

"You know," she said, looking down at Peyton. "Spots are my favorite, too!"

Once again, Briony gasped. "Reawy?"

"Really, really. I love spots."

Oh, Jesus.

It might have been a mistake introducing these two. Not only was my daughter becoming increasingly obsessed with someone who seemed to be a brunette, adult version of her...

No, that was the problem. Peyton was the brunette, adult version of Briony, attitude and all—and if there was anything my daughter didn't need, it was someone who could teach her a thing or ten about sarcasm.

"I'll order pizza," I said, going to stand.

"Oh, you got it last time. I'll go call them." Peyton put her juice on the side table and tried to move, but Briony stopped her.

"No. Mimi told me that only gentlemen buy dinner. Princesses sit and look priddy."

Peyton looked down at her. "Sit and look pretty? I like to buy my own pizza sometimes, and that's okay."

Without missing a beat, Briony said, "Princesses sit and look priddy so the mens buying dinner don't know dat we can kick dere butts."

Then, she grinned.

So, did Peyton.

And I needed to call my mother. Couldn't we teach my daughter to, I don't know, become an engineer or something?

Not that a badass wasn't a totally viable career option, but I didn't know how well that paid.

"Well, that makes sense to me. Is that what we're going to do? Let Daddy buy the pizza, then be pretty, so he doesn't know that we can kick his butt?" Peyton whispered.

Briony nodded. "Oh no, we're missing the moodie."

Peyton looked over her head at me and winked.

It was the sexiest thing I'd ever seen her do, which was weird since I'd seen her with my cock in her mouth. Maybe it was because of the way the curl of her lips made her eyes shine bright.

Or maybe it was because for the first time since Briony became my entire world, there was someone who didn't know her sitting there, being the kind of person she needed in her life.

Fun. Friendly. Crazy. A bright spot of wildness that I, as her father, couldn't really provide.

Even if I was pretty damn good at painting tiny nails.

"Okay, I'll get pizza, and you two look pretty." I stood up.

Briony leaned right against her and looked at me. "Oh, Daddy. We are priddy."

Peyton swallowed a laugh as Briony wriggled her way under her arm and made herself comfortable. She dropped her gaze as my little girl snuggled in against her and squeaked along with the mice.

I dragged myself away before my heart clenched any harder.

Fuck. I preferred it when she couldn't stand the sight of me—when all she wanted to do was yell at me and get away from me.

Fuck and run.

I preferred it when we wanted to fuck and run.

Not watch Cinderella and eat pizza with my tiny human.

I leaned against the wall and, blowing out a long breath, ran my fingers through my hair.

As far as I knew, her experiment was still in place. Sure, it didn't explain why she was here tonight, even though I'd just thrown the idea out since last night and this morning had been cut short. It didn't explain why she was curled up with my baby and watching Cinderella.

I knew the rule. Her golden rule. She had to have sex with someone three times without falling in love with them.

But did that rule include me falling for her?

***

Peyton gently reached over and prodded my arm. I'd had enough of Disney movies around an hour ago, so I was browsing Facebook while she and Briony carried on with their marathon.

If two movies were a marathon, that was.

"She's asleep," Peyton whispered, pointing to where Bri's head was laid on a cushion on top of her lap.

She looked so peaceful and comfortable. She was snuggled right in, eyes closed, even breathing. At least I'd changed her into her pajamas before the pizza had arrived.

"I got her," I whispered back, slowly dislodging her tiny bare feet from my own lap so I could stand.

Gently, I lifted her up, and she wrapped her little arms around my neck, snort-snoring as I disturbed her. I tightly wrapped my arms around her and made sure to be extra careful as I carried her up to her room.

The boards in her room creaked as I expertly swept her covers to the side and set her down in her bed. Her blonde hair directly contrasted against the magenta pillowcase that was covered with tiny, white crowns.

She snuffled a little before she rolled over and quieted.

"Um," Peyton whispered from the door. "I just went to get water and found this on the floor under the table." She held up Briony's beloved Cinderella doll, complete with ketchup stain in her hair. "She told me how much she loves her."

I took the doll from her and kissed her cheek. "Lifesaver."

She blushed and stepped out of the room, disappearing before I could even lay the doll in bed with Briony.

I tucked her right in, kissed her head, and went downstairs after Peyton. I found her sitting on the sofa, cradling a bottle of water, completely enraptured with the live-action Beauty and the Beast.

It was a strange sight, but I didn't say anything. I hovered in the doorway and watched her.

The TV flickered over her features, showing them off to perfection. The gentle curve of her lips and the slight shadow of her eyelashes whenever she blinked. The shadows of her lashes spread out like spiders legs across her skin, and I was mesmerized by how the shadows both shortened and lengthened with each and every blink.

She reached up and tucked some hair behind her ear. One loose lock fell back against her cheek, but she ignored it, throwing her head back to laugh.

Soft. Quiet. Genuine. It sent goosebumps across my arms, and I drew in the quietest deep breath I ever had.

The TV flashed, and in that moment, my memory did the same.

I saw the seventeen-year-old Peyton Marie Austen. Her hair wasn't as long or curly. Her lips weren't in that pink-plum lipstick she adored, and she looked like a baby version of the woman she was now.

And for the first time in ten years, something struck me hard.

Thank fucking God she ignored me. Thank God she never wanted to hear my reason for standing her up. Thank God in ten different languages that she kept her damn stubborn streak.

If she'd listened to me, there was no chance that I'd be looking at her, sitting on my sofa, after spending the last three hours snuggling my daughter and humoring all her questions—and there were a lot of those.

Peyton covered her mouth with her hand as another giggle escaped her, and I couldn't help but smile.

My phone pinged.

She jumped, hand to her chest, and looked over at me. "How long have you been there?"

"Long enough to see you laughing like a little girl at Lumiere."

"He's funny!"

I grinned and pulled my phone from my pocket. Lawrence's name flashed in the message box, and my stomach dropped.

The phrase no news was good news was true.

He never had anything good to say.

"Elliott? Are you okay?" Peyton's brows pulled into a frown, and she reached for the remote.

"I'm fine. I just—gimme a minute, yeah? I'll be right in." I took my phone to the kitchen and opened the message.

Lawrence: Bethany and Vincent are not backing down. Hearing set for three weeks from tomorrow. Will call you tomorrow with specifics.

I wished he'd waited until tomorrow to tell me anything at all.

I let go of a long, heavy breath and sat on one of the chairs.

Just like that, any good feelings I'd had while staring at Peyton like a lovesick puppy disappeared. Completely disintegrated. The space they left was filled with dread.

The sick knowing that I'd done everything for the little girl upstairs, that the only thing I'd ever done for myself was go on that damn blind date, and someone wanted to take her away from me.

I couldn't even be righteous or forceful right now. A hearing date. That made it real. That was a real thing that was happening and signified the start of the single biggest fight of my life.

How could I be thinking about Peyton and falling for her when I didn't even know if I could keep the one girl in my life who was every cell in my body?

"Elliott?"

I looked up, hand rubbing over my mouth. Peyton stood in the doorway, grasping hold of the wooden frame with one pink-nailed hand. Her blue eyes were steady on me, but concern tightened her features.

"Are you okay?"

I could lie. I could tell her yes. I could tell her I'd never been better, and that it didn't matter, there was nothing she could do or say even if it did matter.

"No." The word fell from my tongue so easily. "Not really."

She hovered there for a moment before she pushed off the door toward me. There was a click and the room filled with light. I didn't even know it was dark in here. I'd been so consumed with my phone, I hadn't cared.

Peyton took the chair next to me at the table and rested her hand on my arm. "Do you want to talk about it?"

"No," I said honestly. "But I think I need to."

She lightly squeezed my arm. "Is it about the fight thing you said at my house?"

I tilted my head and met her eyes. "Fight thing?"

"Yeah. Right before you left, you said something about going into the fight of your life and that you couldn't fight for me, too."

I winced. "That came out wrong."

"Maybe. Maybe not. It depends on the fight. If the fight is to pay your electric bill, then I'd be pissed."

The sparkle in her eyes made me smile. It was tiny, but it was a smile all the same.

Man. This wasn't going to be fun.

"Come sit in the front room. This is a long story." I got up, taking her hand. She let me pull her into the room and drag her down onto the sofa next to me. "A few years ago, I met this girl. She was a great girl, and we started to see each other casually. We weren't exclusive, but we reached a place where we were only sleeping with each other. About three months into that, she found out she was pregnant. There was no doubt the baby was mine because of the dates."

Peyton's eyes were wide, but it wasn't shock. She was simply listening to me and looking at me the entire time.

"A couple months later, we broke up. The seriousness of the situation had hit us, and we realized that while we were great at being casual, a serious relationship didn't work for us. She was too wild, and I was too controlled and possessive. She didn't like it, so we called it quits. Nothing changed in terms of the pregnancy. I was there for every doctor visit and when she was born."

I looked down.

"Then, one day, when I was at work when Bri was three weeks old, Jenna went to my parents' house. She left Bri in her car seat with all her things, plus a diary. She told them she wasn't cut out to be a mom, and everything I needed to know was in that journal."

Peyton moved closer to me, and without hesitation, took my hand in hers. Her fingers threaded between mine, long and slender and soft.

"She relinquished parental control not long after that. Bri is one hundred percent mine. I tried to be the good guy and give her parents all that they wanted, but they never visited. They didn't see her or care about her until a few weeks ago." I met her eyes. "But they didn't come to me. They went to their lawyer."

"Oh no," she whispered.

"Yes. They filed for full-time custody. They claim Jenna wasn't in her right mind when she signed Bri over to me, and that she'd benefit more from being in a two-parent family over me alone."

"That's bullshit." Peyton touched her hand to my cheek and made me look at her. "You know that, don't you? Jesus—I've met her twice, and one of those times, she was throwing up. You're the best thing she could ever wish for."

I scratched at my chin and moved away from her to get up. "That text was my lawyer. The initial hearing is set for three weeks' time. I won't have to be there. It's just a presentation of the case, but it's such shit." Both of my hands went into my hair and gripped it. "I never hid her from them. I never tried for one second to keep her from her biological family. Her so-called mom is the one who walked away, not me. She's the one who wrote a fucking journal every day of her pregnancy and documented how much she hated it and Bri. I'm the one who stepped up and has done everything for her ever since she fucking left."

Fingertips. Against my back. They were so gentle.

Peyton trailed her hand across my back until she was standing in front of me. Her ghost of a touch tickled across my hand, then she moved her hand up my arm, over my shoulder, up my neck, until once again, she was cupping the side of my face.

"Elliott," she said in a voice so soft it barely had any volume, "I don't know what to say to you, but I know one thing. You're the most amazing father to her. If anyone looks at you and agrees with her parents, they need to be fired and have all their licenses revoked. Briony needs you, and nothing will ever change that. You've had her for her entire life. She only knows you."

I looked down her, meeting the blue ocean that was her gaze.

Her strong, steely, compassionate gaze that thumped me right in the chest.

"In fact, she's so strong-willed over talking to you through a damn door that if she ever had to leave, I have no doubt she'd break out of a maximum-security prison to find her way back to you. And she's three. That's some Disney princess shit right there."

I placed my hand over hers. "She doesn't know, and she'll never know. She's never asked why she doesn't have a mom because mine is so amazing to her, but that doesn't make it easier. She's mine. I have the papers saying so. But grandparents...they're fucky rights, Peyt. They're so grey they have more shades than that book series."

"Fifty Shades of Grey."

"Right. We're not talking one paint sampler here— we're talking an entire store's worth on a good day."

"Stop," she said softly, placing her other hand on my other cheek. "Stop this."

"I can't. I—"

"Elliott." She closed the distance between our bodies until there was barely a breath between us. "I know you can't. I know you won't stop worrying about this, but as someone who's seen you with her twice, there's no way anyone with half a brain cell will ever take her from you unless it's to feed some freaking ducks or something. She loves you, and you love her more than anything. If they've never seen her, I don't see how they have a claim to custody."

"Neither do I, but that's how this works. They get a fair shot and—"

She pressed her lips to mine. "Stop," she whispered, lips moving against mine with the short word. She pulled back, eyes full of the stubborn determination that once frustrated the hell out of me.

Now? Now, it made me want to stop and listen to her.

"Being angry won't help anything. It doesn't help you or your mom or your dad, and it sure as hell doesn't help Bri." She dropped one hand. The other slid down the sharp line of my jaw, and I swear she rubbed her thumb over the light stubble that coated my chin.

"Did you just rub my stubble?"

"Shut up," she said quickly. "It felt good. Don't judge me."

"No judging." The barest of laughs bubbled inside me. "And for what it's worth, you're right."

She sighed. "Hearing that never gets old."

"Why? 'Cause it's a rarity?"

She smacked her lips. Her glare was hot, but there was nothing really behind it. "Look. Fight of your life or not, I will be the next best thing."

Cute. She thought she wasn't.

"Let's sit again. I promise not to get up again." I pulled her to the sofa with me. She all but fell on top of me, but her ass hit the cushion next to me.

Her legs were both hooked over mine. I stared at them for a moment in anticipation of her moving them, but she didn't.

She kept her legs over mine, her body close to me, and her hand on my arm.

I rested my hand between her legs, halfway up her thighs, and exhaled slowly. "Rationally, I know the truth. I know she's mine. I know there's no reason to take her from me, but that doesn't mean I'm not scared. Who am I if I'm not her father, Peyton?"

CHAPTER SEVENTEEN

PEYTON

There was no greater force than love.
Husbands. Wives. Siblings. Children. Friendships.
Pizza. Wine. Orgasms.
It was all relative.

I DIDN'T HAVE A CHANCE TO ANSWER HIM. HE WAS CAUGHT in a loop, one that reflected on everything he'd ever done as her father. I was by no means privy to his thoughts, but I didn't need to be to know he was replaying almost every second he'd ever spent as her father.

"What do I do if I don't have to wake up at six a.m. to watch re-runs of Paw Patrol or Nella on Nick. Jr?" he asked the TV. "What am I supposed to do for breakfast if I don't have to make chocolate toast with a banana and some grapes?"

I had no answer to that.

But, he had more questions.

Fears. Anxieties. Nightmares.

I set my hand on his firm forearm and, leaning back, looked at him. And listened to him. I sat while he let every single thought burst out of him like a firework display.

Except this display didn't boom in my ears—it boomed in my heart.

"How do I do laundry without getting stains out of unwashable satin dresses? How do I do the grocery shop each week without wondering if she'll want strawberry or chocolate milk this week before bed? Can I even tidy the front room without swearing because I stepped on some tiny plastic thing I don't even identify with? Can I fill the dishwasher if I don't have her plastic plates?

"How would my trash look without fifty boxes of apple juice? Do I know what it's like to buy cake an adult would eat? Or buy yogurt that doesn't have some stupid character on the side? What would I do with the Trolls or Barbie or Disney undies in the wash? Not to mention the one million hair ties I find everywhere from the fridge to the back of the toilet."

"Hair accessories. The bane of women everywhere. The bobby pins multiply like socks lose their pairs," I said.

"Right. What's up with the fucking hair slides? On Saturday, we have a pack of ten matching pairs. On Wednesday, Cinderella is sporting four unmatching ones, Bri has one set, and the rest have been taken by magpies."

"Never buy glitter or shiny ones. That's a life lesson right there for you." I tapped the end of his nose, mostly because I wanted him to look at me. "Honey, you won't have to have any of those fears be your reality, ever. I promise you."

"You can't promise me that, Peyton."

"You need a fake girlfriend? I can pretend we're engaged or something, so the two-parent thing is negated."

His lips curved up. "I promise you, if you ever pretend you're my girlfriend, you'll stop pretending pretty damn soon."

"I think that's a threat," I said slowly. "But I'm not entirely sure. Are all threats bad?"

"Are you trying to distract me?"

"No. If I wanted to distract you, I'd do this." I tugged the neckline of my tank top down, so he could see my cleavage in its full glory. "But, I'm not, so…"

"Whoa, whoa." He stopped me from releasing the fabric. "Don't be drastic. I do need cheering up."

"Elliott Sloane, stop that."

"Stop what? Perving on you? Never."

I pursed my lips, but only because I was trying to hide a smile. I didn't want to be that asshole, but there was a bright glint in his eyes. There was the unmistakable shine of happiness, even though the fear and desperation that obviously tainted him.

Was I the cause of that? Did I bring that tiny smile even though the lines of frustration were still so furrowed in his brow?

Maybe.

Maybe I didn't want to know, even now.

Maybe I wanted to stop thinking, full stop.

I leaned forward and touched my lips to his. "I have to go. I have a call at eight-thirty tomorrow."

"On your cell?"

"Office phone." I moved my legs, but his hand slapped from between my thighs to outside my right one, holding me locked in against him.

"Bri wakes at six-thirty every day," he said, eyes locked onto mine.

"Congratulations. You created a living, breathing alarm clock."

He snorted. "Baby, do you need to go home?"

Baby.

I hated that.

Was that why my heartbeat went funny at the sound of him saying it to me?

"No." It took me a minute, but I finally got it out.

"So, stay. Bri will wake you up. She might make you watch her shows before you've had coffee, but that's a price I'm willing to let you pay."

I leaned back, unable to control the half-smile my lips curled into. "Elliott, I can't stay with you."

"Why not?"

"Every time we've stayed together, we've had sex."

"We stayed together last night and had an intervention the size of your brother between sex and sleep. By the way, the dildo thing? You never explained it?"

Oh. God.

"It was translucent and had a large…head. She thought it was a baby palm tree, and since my bathroom is blue…" I shuddered. "And yes, we did, but still. Sex."

Elliott's eyes held mine in a heavy stare that said so many things but revealed nothing at all. "Peyton, we're not having sex tonight."

"We're not?"

"No. You could fall asleep right now and not wake until midday, but we're not having sex tonight."

My lips were dry. "Why not?"

His fingers were rough. They trailed across my temple to my hairline. Into my hair and the sweeping motion that tucked my hair behind my ear. His eyes followed that slow, smooth movement until his hand had dropped back into his lap and our gazes had collided.

"Because, if we have sex tonight, I don't have a reason to ever see you again."

His words sent a shiver down my spine.

We'd had sex twice.

One more time.

One more, and we were done.

We'd never have to see each other again.

I'd never have to see the guy who never really broke my heart ever again.

I'd never watch princess movies with the cutest girl ever. I'd never eat pizza with him. I'd never watch him wander around shirtless. I'd never see him yell at me for how he felt.

I'd never see him look as if his entire world was inches away from being dropped out from under him.

We'd never kiss. Hug. Touch. Speak.

We'd never acknowledge the other existed.

I'd never get to sit on his sofa and listen to a little, spunky blonde girl tell me everything she knew about the princesses until she was blue in the face.

Why did that terrify me?

Three days ago, I'd hated him.

Was this the consequence of the truth? Did it really distort reality this much? Was perspective truly so screwed by such a tiny lie?

"I'm not in the mood anyway," I said. "I have a headache."

"I have Ibuprofen for that," he said, smiling.

"It's a stress headache. That movie was so far from the original…" I trailed off. "But it's not that late."

Elliott leaned his head back. "So, I'm done talking about my issues. Tell me about Pick-A-Dick."

"Uh…no."

"Why?"

"Because. It's weird. You were the dick that was picked for me, and I'm not sure how I feel about the process."

He laughed, reaching out to me. His fingers slid through my hair, and my scalp tingled. I'd never realized that touching hair was so intimate—I was used to pulling, not touching.

This was that. Touching. A slow, easy touch from hairline to hairline that made me shiver from the sensation of it.

"Well, if my feelings count," Elliott said, running his fingers through to the tips of my hair until the ends fell away onto my chest. "I'm feeling pretty good about it."

I brushed that hair away and, unable to hide my smile, ducked my head the tiniest bit. "Do you really think everything would have changed if I hadn't been an ass to you in school?"

"Yes," he said simply. "I won't lie. I think it would have been, and I didn't lie when I said I feel as though I would have fallen in love with you."

My stomach tightened into knots. "What about now? Are you happy it happened the way it did?"

Slowly, he nodded. "Yeah. I am. If it didn't, we wouldn't be here right now."

"Is that a good thing?"

His gaze collided with mine with a waterfall of honesty and genuine, heart-tugging reality. "Yeah, baby. I think so."

It was, wasn't it?

A good thing.

Despite it all.

This was good.

Now, it was my turn to nod slowly. "What's the time?"

"Almost ten. I usually head to bed around now," Elliott said. "Six-thirty comes quicker than you'd think."

"True. Okay. If I have to stay…"

"You do."

"Let's go."

He finally allowed me to move my legs from his, and I stood and followed him. He left all the boxes and dishes in the room without an iota of concern, and that made me smile, even if a little twitchy.

He also didn't notice the naked Barbie under the coffee table. Or the odd-looking miniature koala by the TV.

I stepped into his room, a cool mix of blues and blacks. Black dominated the furniture fixtures, but the textiles were all blue, with the exception of the floor. That was the same laminate that decorated the rest of the house.

It felt like an after-thought, once that didn't matter as long as princesses and animals existed.

I was alone, so I looked around the entire room. The rug next to his bed was crooked. The lights on the nightstands weren't evenly positioned, and the pillows on the bed were a hot mess.

A TV sat on the dresser at the end of the bed. The remote was on the floor, partially tucked under the bed, and I picked it up so it didn't get lost.

I set it on the nightstand, only to sit on the bed to undress and catch a glimpse of two pairs of his undies and some jeans on the floor on the other side of the bed.

I tossed myself onto my side and looked over. Yep. I was right. Dirty undies and pants.

It made me twitch.

"What are you doing?" Elliott walked in with his shirt off.

My eyes darted across the perfect plains of his muscled torso before I met his gaze. "Your dirty clothes are on the floor. There's dust everywhere."

"Perks of being a builder." He stopped and undid his jeans. They fell from his hips to the floor, and when he stepped out of them, he simply kicked them to the side.

They flew across the floor.

Hit the wall.

Slumped against it.

Don't do it, Peyton. Don't go tidy freak.

"I can't cope with this." I reached over the side of the bed. My hand made instant contact with the dirty clothes. I scooped them up, not caring that his underwear was dirty, and got up from the bed.

The next stop was where he'd kicked off his pants.

"Where's your laundry?" I asked, picking up today's jeans.

He looked at me. Looked away. Back at me. "Bathroom. Next door. There's a big basket in there."

I carried the pile of clothes out of the room, leaving behind his confused but amused expression.

Just like he'd said, there was a laundry basket split into three bags. Black. White. Color.

That made my soul happy.

I divided all the colors out until I noticed that the color section was bulging. My fingers twitched.

I couldn't do his laundry.

I wouldn't do his laundry.

That would be weird.

Wouldn't it?

***

"What are you doing?" Elliott stood in the doorway of his utility room.

It was a tiny room, barely big enough for the washer, dryer, and a sink, but he'd caught me red-handed.

I was pairing his fucking socks, for the love of God.

"Pairing your socks," I said simply. "Your washer and dryer were full, but the basket upstairs was about to overflow."

He looked at me, lips pulled to the side, amusement dancing in his eyes.

"So, I had to wash it," I went on. "But your dryer was full. So, I pulled out the dry stuff, put the wet stuff in the dryer, then put the dirty stuff into the wash."

"That doesn't tell me why I'm watching you fondle my socks."

I was playing with a ball of something, and when I looked down, I saw the folded pair of socks. Immediately, I tossed them to the "ready" pile and cleared my throat.

"I had to fold it," I said simply. "I have issues with laundry."

"You're OCD." He grinned.

"I'm not OCD!" I stood up and put a shirt in the clean pile. "I'm obsessively neat. There's a big difference. I can control my need to be tidy. I just...sleep better with the knowledge there aren't pants on the floor."

Elliott held out both hands. "Well, Peyt, it's been thirty minutes. You don't have to fold my pants while wearing your underwear."

I looked at the pile of laundry.

"But—"

He grabbed me. I was thrown over his shoulder in an instant, and he literally hauled me out of the utility room and up the stairs. I groaned.

It wasn't my fault I was a tidy person, damn it.

He took me right into his room and put me back on the bed. "Did you tidy the living room, too?"

"I might have put the pizza boxes in the kitchen," I replied, refusing to meet eye contact.

"You're OCD."

"I just told you, I'm not. I'm tidy."

"Tidy people don't get eye twitches because of laundry."

"So, I'm really, really tidy." I threw out my arms. "Is that a bad thing? I'm not obsessively clean. I won't start running my fingertips over the top of your TV to check for dust."

He shook his head and got into the bed next to me. "You would not like it if you did."

I jerked around to look at him, alarmed.

He grinned smugly. "Let me guess: you have issues with dust?"

"If I know it's there," I muttered, looking away again. "Everything has a place, and the place for dust is on my cloth."

His laugh sent tingles down my spine. "You're the craziest person I've ever met."

"Why? Because I don't like pants on the floor and dust?"

"And pizza boxes in the living room," he pointed out, moving closer to me and gently coaxing me to lie down.

I did, and he propped his head up on his hand.

"That doesn't make me crazy. It makes me clean."

"And slightly weird in someone else's house."

"You give me orgasms; I clean your house. We both win here. Don't be picky."

He laughed again, this time, leaning down to kiss me. "I'm not complaining. Feel free to come and clean every day if you like."

"Really?"

He paused. "You sound way too excited about that prospect."

I screwed up my face. "I might be a little obsessive. I like cleaning. It's calming. My job is stressful."

"Your job is stressful? Peyton, your job is to look at dicks all day."

"Which would be much more enjoyable if it were porn," I pointed out. "But, I also share a space with my brother and Chloe, and that is stressful. So is finding a man who isn't intimidated by my millionaire client but is driven enough to keep up with her, um, appetite."

"Well," Elliott said slowly. "When you leave me standing in the dust, I could use a nice millionaire to help my legal fees."

"Oh, I don't know if I'm leaving you yet," I replied, meeting his eyes. "At least until I've cleaned your house."

"You're not leaving me?" His lips twitched up. "How are you going to win this bet?"

"Well, the way I see it, there are two options." I held up one finger. "First, we never have sex again."

"How does that solve the problem?"

"I have to have sex with someone three times in two weeks and not fall in love. If we don't have sex, it's void."

"Or he'll make you find someone else to have sex with," he said with an edge to his voice.

Interesting.

"And how does that make you feel?" I asked, teasing.

"How you feel about my pants being on the bedroom floor."

"Ooh. Intense. Maybe we scrap that one." I grinned at him. "The other option that we do it right here, right now, and boom. I win. We're not in love. At least, I know I'm not."

He laughed. "I'm not in love with you, Peyton."

I hesitated. "There feels like there's more to that sentence that you're not saying."

Elliott's eyes met mine. "Yet. I'm not in love with you yet."

Why did my heart skip a beat at that sound?

I didn't want to love him. I didn't want him to love me. Our lives were so different that it seemed so...so...

Weird.

It was easy to be with him. Easy to be with Briony.

But to be in love with him?

It would be too easy, yet too hard at the same time.

"Oh," I said.

"Oh?" His lips quirked to the side. "That's a small response for a big silence."

"I wasn't expecting that," I admitted.

His eyes searched my face. "Does it scare you?"

I looked at him. Did it scare me? I had no control over it, and that scared me. But the idea of it? I may not have wanted him to fall in love with me, but that didn't mean I was scared of the idea.

No. I wasn't scared of Elliott falling in love with me.

I was scared of me falling for him.

I shook my head. "It doesn't scare me."

"I feel like you're the one leaving something unfinished."

"I'm scared that I'll fall in love with you."

"Why?"

"Because your life is so different to mine. And that change is terrifying."

He smoothed my hair away from my face with his roughened fingers. "Falling in love with someone isn't a marriage proposal, Peyton. The only change you'd have to make in your life is that I'm the only person you can have sex with."

I snorted into my hand.

"Because I don't share well," he said through his own laughter. "And just like when someone takes my pizza, I'm liable to get mad."

"I have to admit to being selfish, too. Especially about pizza."

"See? Who knew we'd have that in common?"

I couldn't help but smile at him.

"Seriously, your life doesn't change just because you fall in love with someone. You wouldn't be responsible for Briony just because we'd be in a relationship. Sure, you'd have to listen to her ramble on for hours about ponies and princesses and koala bears. You might have to watch Disney movies—"

"Totally okay with the movies," I interrupted, making him smile.

"—and you might be witness to the occasional hurricane-strength meltdown, but you'd just be fun." His fingers went through my hair again. "You wouldn't be responsible for daycare, or manners, or teaching her wrong from right. None of that would be your responsibility, maybe ever. You'll always have your freedom, Peyt. You're too wild to have your wings clipped."

I swallowed.

How was this fair? How was it that he understood exactly what scared me without me hinting at it?

It was only some ten days ago that I'd walked into that restaurant, sick to my stomach. Angry and confused and hating him.

Now, I was lying in his bed, faced with the very real potential that I was falling in love with him.

"I mean, I'm a little intimidated by the meltdown thing," I said, raising my eyebrows. "Hurricane-strength?"

He grimaced and nodded. "Doesn't happen often, but when it does, we're talking kicking and screaming and fighting. I call it a hurricane tantrum because it's the kind of situation where you make sure she's safe and then hunker down until it passes."

I cough-laughed. "Comparable to Chloe this morning?"

"Like ten Chloes on their period."

I winced. "Ouch. That's...intense."

"You have no idea." He rolled onto his back and checked the time on his phone. "We should sleep."

Sleep? How was I supposed to sleep now?

"Sure." I smiled and pulled the covers right over me. Elliott turned off the light and, after shifting in the bed, pulled me into him. I laid my head on his chest, and he wrapped one arm tight around my body.

"I still can't believe you held that grudge for ten years," he muttered into the darkness.

"I'm a woman. I remember everything. Even the time in science where you passed me a note that said I was pretty, then I balled it up and threw it at you. I didn't want to be pretty. I wanted to learn chemistry."

His whole body shook with silent laughter. "I remember that now. Then, you told me after class that if I was going to hit on you, I should have the balls to hit on you to your face."

"I still stand by that notion. The only notes I want in my life are Post-It notes."

"Peyt?"

"What?"

"You're pretty."

I laughed quietly, tilting my head back. I was just about able to meet his eyes in the darkness. "Thank you," I said quietly. "And you're rather handsome yourself."

"I know," he replied.

I lightly smacked his stomach and snuggled back in. "You're an idiot."

"Yeah, but I'm a handsome idiot."

"Elliott? Go to sleep."

CHAPTER EIGHTEEN

PEYTON

You can't control what somebody else does with their pants.
You can only pick them up and beat them with them.
Whipping, in particular, is effective. And fun.

ELLIOTT STOOD WITH HIS HANDS ON HIS HIPS IN THE living room doorway.

I froze, mid-wipe of the TV. "Um, it was dusty?"

Stoic-faced, he cast his gaze over every inch of the now-clean living room. "Woman, you have a problem."

"Yes. Your ability to dust and do laundry is troublesome," I replied.

"Peyton. It's six a.m. Why are you cleaning?"

I sighed, letting go of the cloth. "I woke up to pee. Your towels were wonky, and one thing lead to another. I did your laundry, too."

"It's six in the morning," he repeated. "When did you pee? Three in the morning?"

"An hour ago." I shifted. "I'm quick."

"Quick? How did you do all of this in an hour?"

"I bleached your toilet, too." I smiled sweetly.

He stared at me, then shook his head and walked into the kitchen. I followed him, but not before I finished wiping off the top of the TV.

Maybe I was a little crazy.

"Are you mad?"

Elliott burst out laughing, grabbing a mug. "Peyton, you just cleaned my house. I'm not mad, I'm confused."

"Why are you confused?"

"Because. I find it hard to reconcile the outspoken, sexy woman I know with this frantic mess who can't stand having dirty pants on the floor."

"I don't exactly shout my...quirk...to the world." I put the cloth in the sink and leaned against the side. "We all have something we keep to ourselves, and the cleaning thing is mine. Most people just think I'm an exceptionally tidy person because I'm a control freak."

"You're not a control freak?"

"You think I'm a control freak?"

"You're a little control freakish," Elliott admitted. "The first time we slept together? You literally dictated to me how it had to go."

"And you followed orders exceptionally well."

His lips twitched. "It's not a bad thing. You like everything just so."

"You don't think it's weird that I started folding your laundry last night?"

"Oh no, it's weird." He laughed, wrapping his arms around my shoulders. "But it's a good kind of weird. And I kind of want to ask if you know how to get juice out of a satin dress."

"Uh..." I awkwardly pointed to the sink. "I saw it. It's soaking."

Elliott looked at the pink dress submerged in weird-colored water. "What is that?"

"A trick Mimi taught me when I was a teenager. Mom always used to send Dom's sports stuff over to get to get the stains out."

He swung his gaze back to mine, looking like he'd just had an epiphany. "I don't even know what to say to you. Are you sure you woke up at five?"

"Maybe four-thirty," I reluctantly said. "I couldn't sleep."

"You, woman, are a wonder, aren't you?"

"I don't know what you mean, but it sounds like a compliment, so I'll say thank you."

Elliott grinned, then kissed me. "Thank you for cleaning my house. I hate cleaning."

Huh. Maybe this whole thing wasn't so crazy after all.

"Just... don't go in Briony's room, okay?" There was a mischievous glint in his eyes as he said that and released me.

"Why? What's in there?"

"Toys. Lots of toys."

My eye twitched.

He grinned.

Damn it.

Just as I was about to respond, Briony herself appeared in the kitchen doorway, rubbing her eyes. "Is it morning time?" she asked in a sleepy tone.

"It is morning time," Elliott confirmed. "How did you sleep?"

"I slept lots," she replied. "Can I had bekfast now?" she caught sight of me. "Peydon!"

She rushed me and hugged me before I could react.

I laughed and stroked her hair. "Good morning to you, too."

She dropped her head back and grinned up at me. "Hiya. Daddy, can I had bekfast, pwease?"

"You can," he replied with a smile. "What would you like?"

She pursed her lips and tapped her finger on them. "Ah-ha! Chocwat toast and a nana, pwease, Daddy."

His lips curved up, and I got the feeling this was a daily occurrence between them.

"You got it. Go sit at the table, and I'll make your breakfast for you."

"Okay." She trotted off, dragging Cinderella by the foot.

"Every morning," Elliott sighed, turning to where the toaster was.

I smiled, watching the muscles of his back flex as he put two slices of toast in.

"What are you doing today?" he asked, facing me again. "I was going to take Briony out somewhere."

"I have to work." I toyed with my hands. "Apparently, people still need to get laid on Sundays."

"The horror."

"It's a hard life, but someone has to make it happen." I shrugged. "But I'm a little twitchy about her room."

"Feel free to clean it whenever you like."

"Goddamn tonight being girls' night," I muttered, taking a mug out of the cupboard.

He laughed. "Ah, freedom. It sounds terrible."

I pursed my lips and looked at him. No matter how hard I tried, I had to smile.

Idiot.

***

"I'm falling in love with him. There. I said it."

Chloe and Mellie both stared at me, jaws slack. I nodded. I knew it. Elliott knew it. Hell, Briony maybe even knew it, but I needed to say it out loud to make it real.

"No, no, no, no." Mellie got up from the sofa and walked over to me. "No, no, Peyton. You're not staying on the plan."

Chloe came quickly behind her. "You hate him."

"I did, then I found out the truth."

"Ignore the truth!" Mellie flapped her hands at me. "Ignore the truth, Peyton!"

"Don't you think I tried?" I ground my teeth and grabbed the pitcher of margarita. "I didn't want this to happen, okay? But, I can't help it. He's an amazing person, and no matter how hard I try to ignore it, it's the truth."

Chloe wound her fingers in her hair. "This is bad. This is very bad. If Dom is right, we'll never live it down. Oh God, I'll have to hear about it every day for the rest of my life."

"We could kill him off," Mellie suggested, filling her glass back up.

"That's a little drastic over five hundred dollars," I replied.

"How much is your pride worth, Peyton?" Chloe shoved her finger in my face. "Is it worth listening to me whine and complain about his gloating forever? Is it worth knowing that in the biggest dare of your life, you lost?"

This escalated quickly.

"We're gonna have to kill him off." Mellie sighed. "I watch enough TV. We could probably get away with it."

"You're not killing anybody," Jake said, walking into the kitchen.

"You're a funny looking girl," I said to him.

He gave me a weary look and turned to Mellie. "You're not killing anyone. No matter how good your plan is, you'll trip over something and get caught. Likely kill yourself."

I didn't often agree with Jake, but in this case, he was right. Even Chloe was already nodding her head in agreement.

"Three days, Jacob. It's been three days since I tripped over." She pointed to the board on the fridge that bore a big number three in red.

"Only just. You almost fell over your sweater this morning."

"Which is why I tell you to pick them up, Melanie," I said. "So you don't trip."

"When did this go from Peyton fucked up to pick on Mellie?" She huffed, taking a big mouthful of drink.

Chloe pointed at Jake. "Your clumsiness is the only thing they ever agree on. You should have barred him from the house."

"I live here," Jake pointed out. "Mostly to stop Mellie from seriously hurting herself on a daily basis."

That was true, too.

"Can we get back to Peyton fucked up?" Mellie asked.

"What did you fuck up?" Jake looked at me. "Did you finally match my cousin to someone?"

"No, and please tell him to stop sending me dick pics. The next one to land in my personal inbox is being photoshopped to be three inches smaller, printed out, and pinned to posts through the city with his phone number." I titled my glass in his direction as he laughed. "No, I started to fall in love."

"You're in love?" His eyebrows shot up.

"Not in love. Falling. And there's no need to sound so surprised."

Jake slowly nodded. "There is. You don't do love. Mellie does. We all know Chloe is in love with your brother—"

"I am not in love with him!" she shouted.

"—But you, Peyton? No. I've never seen you come remotely close to falling in love."

I would have argued, but it was so true it hurt.

"Well, Tweedledumb and Tweedledick over here," I nodded toward the girls, "decided that the guy I should sleep with for Dom's dickhead challenge was my high school crush."

Mellie held up a finger. "Who you hated. For ten years."

Jake quirked an eyebrow. "I'm no expert, but that's quite the one-eighty."

I stared at him flatly. "I found out that what I thought he did to me wasn't how I saw it. You won't be surprised to hear I ignored him whenever he tried to tell me the truth in school."

He shook his head. He was not surprised at all.

"When it was all cleared up as a stupid and naïve misunderstanding—although I still don't know who egged my car—it was easy to see him differently." I paused. "Plus, there's something really hot about a guy looking after a little girl."

"Is he a nanny?"

"He's a father," I said. "His daughter is three."

"And part of the reason she has her thong in a twist," Chloe helpfully added. "She's great with kids, but not so much with being restrained."

Hey, now.

Jake folded his arms across his chest. "Why does that bother you? Presumably, you've met? You get along?"

"She loves me," I said honestly. "And I might even love her right back, but there's so much responsibility. Plus, her maternal grandparents have launched a custody battle. Elliott said none of that would be my responsibility, but it would be. There's no way I couldn't not get invested. What would I do if I saw her doing something wrong and he wasn't there? Just not say anything? Of course, she'd be my responsibility if we were in a serious relationship."

"Whoa," Chloe said. "Custody?"

"It's a long story. Her mom gave up her rights, but they want her. That's the general gist of it." I shrugged and finished my drink.

Mellie immediately poured me a new one.

"Do you mind if I tell you what I think? As someone who doesn't mind pissing you off?" Jake asked.

"Go ahead. Someone needs to give it to me straight, I guess."

"I don't think your reservations about his daughter are about the responsibility side of it at all. Or even the custody battle."

I stared at him, confused.

"I think it's about you. A child is such a huge departure from your life right now, and it's not the restraint or the life change or anything like that. If it was, you'd be walking away without a second thought."

He had a point.

"He has a point," Chloe added.

"Peyton, I think it's all about you." Jake shrugged. "I think you're using that as an excuse, but what you're really worried about is the fact that little girl will look up to you. You'll be her role model. Everything you do, she'll do. She'll copy you in the way kids tend to do. Sure, you might not have to teach her right from wrong and all that stuff, but you'll be teaching her how to be a woman, and that's a huge task."

I swallowed.

Of all the people to hit the nail on the head, why did it have to be him?

"I'm not good enough to be anybody's role model." I ran my fingers through my hair. "Especially not hers. She needs stability and someone who knows how to teach her to do all the things she needs to know."

"Peyt..." Mellie sighed.

Jake shook his head at her, then met my eyes. "While your job choice is more amusing to me than anything, and I tend to find myself in a state of constant annoyance around you, you've missed the mark entirely. You're not good enough to be anyone's role model? My God, Peyton? Can you hear yourself?"

I bit the inside of my cheek.

"You run your own business. You own your house. You own your car. You're strong and independent. You don't allow anyone to take advantage of you. You're headstrong and determined. You're ambitious, and you don't settle for anything less than the best. But, you're also compassionate and supportive, and you would drop anything to help the people you love." Jake held out his hands. "You're a pain in my fucking ass, but you're one hell of a woman, Peyton Austin. That little girl would be lucky to have you as her role model."

My lips parted, but no words came out. Instead, I swallowed and looked down at the table.

We were oil and water in terms of our ability to get along, so to hear that from him?

It was a punch to the gut with a heavy dose of reality.

"Think about it," he said, softer. "You don't have to rush into anything, and if this Elliott is a decent guy, then he'll understand that. Sounds like he already does." He turned to Mellie and kissed her. "I'm going to meet Sam. I'll see you later."

"Okay." She smiled. "Have fun."

"Bye, girls." He waved, then left us to it.

Silence filled the room. I was pretty sure I'd just had my ass handed to me in the best possible way.

And I hated to admit it, but he was right. I was all of those things, but that didn't mean I was any less daunted by the prospect of something real happening with Elliott.

That didn't mean I was any less afraid.

"Are you okay?" Mellie asked, hovering as if she wanted to come to me.

"Yeah." I frowned. "I'm okay. I think."

"You think?" Chloe questioned. "Think isn't really enough."

"I'll be fine," I amended my answer to. "Seriously, guys. It's okay. Jake's right. It's more than all of those things. I think I'm just overwhelmed by it all."

Mellie filled all of our glasses, and we went to sit back in the living room. "What overwhelms you?"

"Ooh, I know! Dick pics." Chloe grinned.

She wasn't wrong.

My lips turned up into a small smile. "Nailed it, Chlo. So many dick pics."

"You're the one who made that part of the process."

"Right, but how can you pick a dick without seeing the dick?"

"Can we stop saying dick?" Mellie looked between us. "Seriously. That's enough dick."

"There's a thing as enough dick?" I asked, grinning.

"Yes. Believe it or not," Chloe muttered. "It's when you work with Dom."

All three of us laughed.

And, for the rest of the night, nobody mentioned Elliott, Briony, or falling in love.

It was amazing.

CHAPTER NINETEEN

PEYTON

Some things transcended time without ever getting old.
Disney. Dolls. My Little Pony.
The total agony of stepping on fucking Lego.

ELLIOTT BLINKED AT ME. "WHAT DID YOU DO?"

I bit my tongue, that was what I did. And it should have been celebrated.

"Lego," I squeaked, holding onto my foot. "Ouch. Hurts."

Understanding brightened his expression. "Oh."

"Oh? Oh! That's your reaction?"

He held up his hands. "Peyt, you decided to clean her bedroom. Where there are children, there are pieces of Lego just waiting to be stepped on. Lego is timeless. Sadly," he added, bending over to pick up the offending piece of plastic.

"I need industrial-level boots to clean this!"

"She usually tidies it herself," he said as he threw the Lego into its box. "She gets annoyed if I tidy it because I do it wrong."

"So? Why is she letting me do it?"

"Well, I did ask."

"And?" I gingerly touched my foot to the carpet.

Elliott sighed. "She said you're allowed to tidy her room because she likes you, and because you're a girl like her, which means it'll get done properly, unlike when a stupid boy does it."

I toyed with wanting to laugh, but he looked so drained by that statement I decided not to. "She's been listening to your mom again, huh?"

With a grimace, he nodded. "I really have to talk to her about it."

"It's a good thing. Mostly. She'll grow up to be fierce." I shrugged. "If fierce is the worst attribute she has, everyone wins."

"Great. I'm going to end up with two of you." He flung his hand in my direction.

"Hey." I put my hands up, holding a stuffed doll. "I can go at any time. Her, you're stuck with. Me? Not so much."

"You're not allowed to go." His eyes sparkled. "At least, not until you've cleaned the room."

I folded my arms. "It all makes so much sense. You don't want me. You want my cleaning habits."

"Right now? Yes. I think I just saw a week-old slice of banana." He wrinkled his face up.

"Wow. Talk dirty to me, Elliott."

"I just did. Literally dirty." He moved a plastic carriage and picked up a black sludgy mess. "Yep. Week-old banana."

I flattened myself against the wall and winced. "Kids are gross."

"Welcome to my world."

"Your world is gross."

"And glittery. Gross and glittery," he reminded me.

No. Actually, I was the one who was glittery. I'd been attacked by a small pot of glitter that didn't have its lid on properly.

I'd be washing that off my scalp for weeks.

"Yeah, you're gross, and I'm glittery," I said when he came back in.

"It's kind of like Beauty and the Beast," he mused.

"Except, I'm the one who got cursed, because this glitter will never come out of my hair."

He looked at my hair and started laughing. "It suits you, though. Bright blue is your color."

I gave him a totally flat look. I was seconds away from telling him to go fuck himself when Briony's footsteps on the stairs echoed up to us.

"Daddy? Daddy. Daddy." She stopped in the doorway. "Daddy."

"Yes, princess?" he replied.

"I drank all the juice," she said. "And I can't reached another."

"I'll get you a juice if you help Peyton finish putting your toys away," Elliott bargained. "Because you've had two since you got home, so that's more than enough for now."

Briony sighed. "Okay, Daddy. I help."

She immediately got stuck in, going to the little Barbie house in the corner. There was a pink tub next to it, and she enthusiastically picked up all the dolls and the clothes to put them away.

She moved even quicker than I did, assorting all her toys into their rightful homes until the floor was clear of them. All that was left behind was an empty apple juice, a popsicle stick, and what looked to be a Reese's mini squished into the rug.

Elliott took care of the rug, rolling it up with a mutter about not remembering being that dirty as a kid, causing me to bite back a laugh.

Briony put a snow globe on the windowsill and looked over at me. "Are we done, Peydon?"

"I have to mop the floor, but nearly." I smiled.

"Oh, okay. I had a question."

"Sure. What's your question?"

Shyness flickered over her features as she looked at the floor. "Are you and Daddy fwends?"

"We are friends," I said slowly. I walked over to her and crouched down. "What's up, Bri?"

"Are you donna stay fwends? 'Cause, 'cause, Peydon," she finally looked up at me, "I like hading you here."

I pushed her hair out of her eyes. "I think we will stay friends, yeah. He's quite funny, isn't he?"

She nodded. "And he gives the bestest huggies."

"I agree with you." I tapped her nose and noticed how her hair fell back in front of her eyes. "You need a haircut."

Another nod. "Daddy forgotted." She pushed it out of the way again.

"Do you have a hairclip?"

"In dere." She pointed at a jewelry box with Cinderella on.

I opened it up and found a whole drawer full of hairclips. I pulled out two, then went to Briony and clipped her bangs out of her eyes. "There. Is that better?"

She beamed up at me. "Bedder. Fank you, Peydon."

"You're very welcome. I'll make sure you get your hair cut."

She gasped. "Are you donna taked me?"

Was I? Was that what I'd offered?

Not in adult speak, but in toddler speak.

Yep. I had.

"Sure," I said with a half-smile. "I'll take you."

"Fank you!" She grabbed me into a tight little hug. Meaning she wrapped her arms so tightly around my neck that I could barely breathe.

"Okay," I wheezed, extracting myself from her. Man, she was surprisingly strong. "I'm gonna go find the mop. Can you pick up the trash and put it in the trashcan?"

She swung her head side to side to look for the trash. "Okay. I can dood dat."

I got up and went downstairs. Elliott was hiding in the kitchen with a cup of coffee, and he looked guiltily up when he saw me.

"I was just…taking a break," he said.

I raised an eyebrow. "Well, while you were taking a break, I got roped into taking your daughter for a haircut."

He stopped, the mug halfway to his mouth. "Why would you agree to that? You know she has to sit still, right? Have you ever tried to get a three-year-old to sit still?"

"And that's why she needs it cut, then," I muttered.

"How did you manage to agree to that?"

"I didn't. I said I'd make sure she got it cut, and apparently, in toddler-speak, that means "I'll take you to get your hair cut."" I shrugged and got some water from the fridge. "She asked if I was going to take her. I couldn't say no, could I?"

Elliott sipped from the mug. "You could have. You have no self-control."

I stared at him flatly. "You should be glad of that. If I had self-control, I never would have slept with you."

"Sex and haircuts for a toddler are totally different things."

"I absolutely hope they are, or I want to get off this planet." I looked at him pointedly and sipped from my water. "I can take her. I don't mind."

"There goes your fear of responsibility. Look at you, tackling it head-on."

"It's taking your child to the hair salon or breaking her heart."

"Breaking her heart might be easier on your nerves. Seriously. Trying to get a three-year-old to sit still is akin to herding cats. You might even get the scratches." He was deadly serious. "Mom usually cuts her hair, but I guess she didn't notice."

I rolled my eyes and recapped my water. "You're a drama queen. It'll be fine. So what if she wriggles a lot? The stylists are used to it."

"You're brave," he muttered. "Very brave."

"I allowed my friends to set me up on a blind date. Of course, I'm brave."

"We'll reevaluate that soon. After the haircut." He winked and toasted me with his cup.

"Peydon!" Briony shouted from upstairs. "I gedded the trash! I bringed it now!"

Little stomps echoed as she came downstairs. She'd found an empty packet of goldfish, too, and she had everything clutched tight in her little hands. She walked to the trashcan and dumped everything in it.

"Are you donna mop soon?" she asked me, staring up at me with her big, blue eyes.

"Just having a drink and I'll be right there," I said.

"Okay. Das good." And off she went, back up the stairs again.

Elliott was staring after her. "Did she just pick up trash without throwing a tantrum?"

I held up my hands. "I said please and asked nicely. I can be reasonable, and it usually works."

"Huh. I sometimes ask nicely five times, and she can't hear a word I say until I shout."

"Selective hearing. Women do that when men are talking crap."

He finished the coffee and put the mug on the side. "I have got to call my mother."

"Good luck with that. Where's your mop?"

"A mop? Why would I have a mop?"

No. He didn't have a mop?

"To clean your floors that aren't carpet," I explained as if I was talking to an idiot.

Actually, it felt an awful lot like I was.

Who didn't own a mop? Mimi had four. Hell, even Dom owned a mop. Not that he probably knew how to use it, but he had one.

"Don't have one," he said nonchalantly. "Doesn't a sponge do the same job?"

I held up a finger. "I might like Cinderella, but I'm not scrubbing a floor on my knees. Go buy me a mop. I'll wait." I folded my arms.

He grinned. "Calm down, firecracker. I have a mop in the utility."

"You're a dick. A giant, huge, shit-talking dickdouche."

"It's so nice when you show me you care," he drawled. "It's in the corner, behind the dryer. I don't use the mop, clearly."

I stuck my middle finger up at him and went into the utility. There was a black pole in the corner, so I reached over and grabbed it.

It was stuck.

I leaned over the dryer. It was stuck in a bucket that moved, but the mop itself was solid and glued to the bottom of the bucket.

I sighed. Thank god this was a front-loader.

I climbed up on top of it and reached down to get the bucket. I narrowly avoided smacking myself in the head with the mop handle as I lifted it and jumped down. It didn't smell great, so I held it at arm's length as I carried it into the kitchen.

Elliott was on his phone, and again looked up when I walked in. "What are you doing?"

I handed him the bucket. "That needs to be cleaned out before I touch it."

"Why do I have to do it? You're the neat freak." His lips twitched.

"Because this is literally disgusting, and since you have a child, you're used to cleaning up disgusting messes. The worst thing I've ever cleaned is bird poop off my car."

He sighed, putting down his phone. He took the bucket from me and looked inside. The disgusted expression he made said it all.

"Gross. This is why I don't mop." He put it in the sink and turned on the tap.

"Well," I said, standing next to him and nudging his elbow. "If you mopped, this wouldn't happen."

He nudged me right back. "Don't be a smartass."

"Can't help it." I nudged him again. "It's in my DNA."

He nudged me harder.

"What was that for?" I asked, knocking my elbow against his arm.

"Stop nudging me." Elliott did it again.

"Stop nudging me," I argued with another nudge.

"You started it." Nudge.

"I don't care. Finish it." Nudge.

He nudged me without speaking.

I nudged him right back.

Nudge.

Nudge.

Nudge.

I pushed his arm and stepped away. "Ugh, stop it."

He walked toward me and grabbed my hands.

I raised my eyebrows. "What are you doing?"

"Stopping you from nudging me."

I brought my right foot up and kicked his butt.

"You did not—you kicked me!" Elliott's jaw dropped, but there was laughter in his eyes. "What the hell, Peyton?"

"You stopped me from nudging you. What, did you think I'd just stand here and let you imprison me with those nice arms of yours?"

"You like my arms?"

"I said they're nice, but lots of things are nice. Avocado on toast? Nice. UGG boots? Nice. It's nothing special."

He tugged me right into him, snatching me fully in his arms when my body hit his. I let out a little "oomph" as he circled me with his strong arms and held me in place.

"Like them now?" He looked down at me.

"They're nice. What else do you want me to say?"

"Peyton, nice is what guys say when they're so fed up with shopping but want to get laid. Nice isn't even close to a compliment. I tell Bri things are nice that I probably never even listened to."

"Harsh. She has a lot of things to say!"

"Which is why they get tuned out after a while. That's parenting for you, baby."

Eh, I got it. I tuned out Chloe and Mellie all the time, and what with Chloe's schtick with my brother and Mellie's clumsiness, that sometimes felt like parenting.

"Okay, fine. Whatever. Let me go now." I patted his chest. "Please."

He shook his head. "Not for a second."

"Why? This isn't a particularly enjoyable hug. You're standing on my foot."

Laughing, he moved his foot. "Sorry. I didn't know."

"Yeah, well, my toes do," I whined.

"Sssh." He leaned his face closer to mine. "I have a question."

"Oh no, not another. The last time I heard that from someone in your family was when your daughter asked me if we're "fwends.""

He leaned back, eyebrows raised. "She did that?"

"Upstairs."

"What did you say?"

"I said we were friends."

"What did she say?"

"She asked me if we'd be "fwends" for a long time."

His eyes flashed with something, and he tilted his head to the side. His fingers tickled across my arm before he said, "And what did you say?"

"You're terrible at nonchalance," I said. "And I told her that I thought we might be friends for a long time, yes."

"And by friends, you mean…"

I smacked his chest, and he let me go. "You know what I mean. Hell, I got talked into taking her to the hair salon—a trip I doubt you're going to accompany me on—so I may as well."

"May as well?" He grinned. "Boy, that's enthusiastic, Peyt."

"Daddy? Why is the warder on the floor?"

We both jumped.

Where the hell did she come from?

We turned around and looked at the sink. Water was overflowing out of the mop bucket and over the edge of the counter onto the floor.

"Damn it!" Elliott jumped into action. Right as he reached the bucket, the mop handle swung down and hit him on the head.

Briony burst into tinkling laughter that made me laugh even harder.

"You little—" Elliott cut himself off before he swore and grabbed the handle. He'd barely turned off the tap when he handed me the mop. "It got unstuck," he said cheerily, grinning.

I wrinkled up my face and took the mop. "Gross, Elliott. Gross."

"Ew, Daddy! It's yucky!" Briony pinched her nose. "Ewww!"

"Elliot! Take it away!"

He sighed and put it back in the sink. He slowly tipped the bucket water into the sink, so he could wash out the mop.

Five minutes, soap, and hot water later, the mop was clean, and the bucket had lost all yucky bits of residue. Briony had subsequently gotten bored of him trying to clean it, grabbed some chips, and gone into the front room to color.

"There." He handed me a full bucket of hot, soapy water, and the now-clean mop.

"Thank you. Finally." I took them.

He pursed his lips, but the corners twitched with his smile. "Shut up."

I took the bucket and mop upstairs to Briony's room and started cleaning. Halfway through, I felt hands on my hips, and I was pulled back into a hard body.

I twisted my head and craned my neck up. "What are you doing?"

"Friends, huh?" Elliott said quietly.

"Friends. I didn't want to have to explain to your daughter the birds and bees."

He nodded, releasing me. "Good choice. But…What are you going to tell Dom?"

I stopped, sighing, and leaned on the mop. "I haven't figured it out yet. I'm sure I will. After I've stopped by the bank for his five hundred dollars."

He snorted, glancing down quickly. "I'm kinda glad you were my blind date."

"I'm kinda glad you were mine." I walked across the room, dragging the mop with me, and kissed him slowly. He wrapped one arm around my waist, and my heart beat a little faster when he sighed as we parted.

"How do we do this?" he asked, looking into my eyes.

"Same way we have been. I guess we'll figure it out as we go."

"I guess we will." He cupped the back of my neck and kissed me again.

This one was deeper, and more real, and it made all the hairs on my arms stand on end.

It was perfection.

***

"This belongs to you." I put five hundred dollars in fifties on Dom's desk.

He looked down from his computer at the stack of bills. "What?"

I dropped into his client chair. "Five hundred bucks. You won, Dom."

He stared at me for a long second. "What? I don't get it. You fell for him?"

I sighed and ran my hands through my hair. "Yeah. Falling. Whatever. There are some very real feelings there, and we've decided that we're going to try to make a relationship work. So, there you go. Your winnings, bro." I put one finger on top of the fifties and slid it across the desk closer to him.

"I don't understand, Peyt. How did that happen?"

"The first night worked, then the second time, Briony was sick. I stayed to help him clean up—"

"Of course."

"—And after that, things kind of snowballed. The other day? When you came for the expenses? We'd just had a massive fight, where he left, and I chased him barefoot down the street."

"You chased him barefoot down the street?" Dom's eyebrows shot up. "Seriously? You chased somebody?"

I shrugged. "I wasn't done talking, and he was leaving."

"Well, now that makes sense. You'd swim the Mississippi if you thought someone there was ignoring you."

True story.

"Anyway, one thing led to another. That was the night I found out what happened in high school— which I'll tell you later—and it made me acknowledge the feelings I'd been ignoring anyway." I rested my head on my hands. "So, congrats. You win. I was not able to sleep with someone three times without falling in love with them."

"I could have told you that." He snorted and picked up the money.

"Is Chloe here yet?" I pushed the chair back to get up.

"No, she's avoiding me."

"Imagine that." I rolled my eyes. "It's all good. I'll call her." I tossed him a wave and walked through the hall to my office.

I sat down at my computer and fired it up. My to-do list was ten miles long, but at least I'd gotten that covered.

I turned to retrieve a file on a client from the cupboard behind me, and when I turned, there was five hundred dollars on my desk.

I looked at the money and up to my brother. "What are you doing?"

"I can't take this money, Peyton."

"Sure, you can. You won."

"Not fairly." Dom put his hands in the pockets of his navy chinos and looked at me. "We didn't set clear boundaries. I agreed based on it being a complete stranger. You already had an emotional attachment to Elliott when this started. You were never going to be able to separate sex and emotion. So, 'cause of that, it's a tie."

"Are you messing with me?"

He shook his head. "It doesn't feel right. I'm not happy about beating you here. Plus, you know. He gave me an ass-kicking over the way I spoke to Chloe, so." He shrugged. "He's a good guy, and I'm glad you finally got your closure."

My lips formed a slow smile. "See? Why can't you be this nice to Chloe?"

"She pisses me off."

"Because you have a crush on her. I know you do. I saw your face when she told you she used to have one on you."

Dom tried to argue, but all that came out was a frustrated breath. He threw himself down onto the chair. "She just—I just—shit."

"And there's the admission I was waiting for." I smirked. "Dom, either tell her how you feel or move on. There's no use holding onto those feelings if you're never going to act on them."

"I can't tell her. She'll bury me alive, Peyt. She hates me. No. I think the best thing to do is offer to set her up with someone as an apology for how I've been the last couple of months."

No. No. Don't do that.

"What exactly will that achieve?" I tucked the money into my purse.

"She gets to date someone good enough

for her, and I'll see how happy she is, and I'll be able to get rid of this little crush. In theory." He stood and waved his arms lamely.

"What if she sets you up with someone right back?"

"Good. It'll be good. She should do that. I'll suggest that, too."

That went wrong.

"What? Why do you look like I just killed your cat?"

"I just think it's messy," I said a little too high-pitched. "Two matches? Plus, all your work now? Hooooey, Dom. That's a lot of work."

"Peyt, you said it yourself. She's too good for me."

"I say a lot of things when I'm angry. I don't always mean them."

"Do you know something I don't?"

"No! No. I'm like Jon Snow. I know nothing. Nothing, I tell you." I mimicked a cross being drawn over my heart with my finger.

Dom stared at me for a moment. "I'll think about that. But, I think it's a good idea."

Instead of saying anything else, I simply nodded, smiled.

And banged my head on the table the second he'd left.

What. A. Mess.

EPILOGUE

ELLIOTT

The best things in life were free.
Except for pizza and beer.
And lawyers. They were most definitely not free.

THREE WEEKS LATER

MY THROAT WAS THICK AS I GOT OUT OF MY CAR.

I stared up at the house that I loved, the one where Bri and I had lived in for almost her entire life. I leaned back against the side of the car and locked it, and just stared a little more.

The idea that she might not live there anymore was terrifying. The thought that two people who knew nothing about her could take her from me was beyond comprehension.

That was a hole that not even Peyton would be able to fill.

And I was so thankful she'd never have to try.

I blew out a long breath and gave my shoulders a shake, dislodging the stress I'd felt as I'd waited in the courtroom. I hadn't wanted to be inside, but I couldn't not be there at the same time.

Luckily for me, Dad had skipped on another fishing trip, so Mom had been all too happy to hang out here with Peyton and Briony while I went.

I walked into the house and into the living room. Peyton was sitting on the sofa. Her feet were up on the coffee table, covered in taco-printed socks. She was typing furiously with Nick Jr. on the TV on mute.

I cleared my throat.

She jerked her head up, her eyes finding me instantly. "You're back."

I looked at her flatly.

"Elliott?" She pushed the computer to the side and stood up.

"Where's Bri?"

"She's baking cookies with your mom in the kitchen. She got some new Disney cutters. Something about Mickey cookies? I don't know." She wrung her hands in front of her. "How are you?"

"I'm okay." I stuffed my hands in my pockets and immediately took them back out.

"How did it go?" Worry tainted her features, and I knew I couldn't keep this up for much longer.

I was already feeling guilty that she was so worried, and I had the best news.

"It went well," I answered, watching her face.

"Well? What happened?"

"The judge threw the case out."

Her mouth opened and closed like a fish's, and the finger she tried to point at me twitched in confusion at the same time. "He threw it out?"

I grinned and nodded. "He said they had no basis to request full-time custody. I'd been reasonable in allowing them free contact that they'd never participated in, and he suspected an ulterior motive regarding Jenna. He said I'm obviously a great father, and there are no problems with Briony or her health or her development. Taking her away from me, even partially, would do nothing but hurt—"

I couldn't even finish the sentence, because Peyton launched herself at me with a scream. Her legs hooked around my waist, and she buried her face in my neck as she hugged me. I had to stagger back a few steps to steady myself, but I hugged her back and laughed.

Mom came running into the room. "What happened? Who died? Why is there screaming? Are we being robbed?"

"What's robbed, Mimi?" Briony asked.

I looked at Mom. "The case was thrown out."

Mom touched her hands to her mouth. Her eyes filled with tears, and she fanned her face with her tears. "Oh."

Peyton slid down my body and sniffed. I glanced down at her. She had tears escaping her eyes, and I reached out to wipe one away.

"Why are you crying, you silly fool?"

"I'm so happy," she whispered, leaning into me.

I wrapped one arm around her and kissed the top of my head as Mom came to hug me, too.

Briony frowned. "Who frowed out a case? I not allowed to frow fings, am I, Daddy?"

"No. No, you're not, princess."

"So, why is everyone happy someone frowed somefing out? I confused."

Mom laughed, and she covered her mouth once again. "Never you mind, Little Miss Sherlock. Let's go finish those cookies, huh? We're almost done."

"Okay. Can we cutted Minnie ones, too?"

"We sure can!" Mom ushered her out of the room with a wink at us, and the second she was gone, Peyton turned her body into mine and pressed her face to my chest.

I wrapped both arms around her body, resting my chin on top of her head. I took a deep breath and let it go again, briefly closing my eyes to just take in this moment.

She sniffed and pulled back slightly. "So, will they appeal?"

"The judge said that if they had two brain cells to rub together, they wouldn't. There's no judge in this country who, in his right mind, would take a little girl away from the only life she's ever known. He also reminded them that their daughter was the one to willingly sign away her rights, and despite their claims, we had proof. One of the things she left me was a psych evaluation. She was in her right mind at the time the decision was made. He offered for them to try partial or visitation, but he said he'd deny both if it landed across his desk again."

"Why visitation?"

"Because of the way they handled this without ever seeing her. He doesn't believe unsupervised visits are the way forward because he doesn't trust them."

"Just like you don't."

I nodded. "But, it's done now. The last three months of stress has been worth it."

Peyton smiled up at me with watery eyes. "I'm so happy for you." She kissed the corner of my mouth, letting her forehead rest against my chin.

I tilted my face down. "Me, too. But, I'm also happy for us."

"Me, too." She looked up, and our lips met for a soft kiss.

"Peyt?" I said, brushing hair away from her face.

"Mhmm?"

"I have to tell you something."

She blushed and cupped the side of my face. "I love you, too."

"I was going to say your mascara is running, but I'll take that."

"Damn it, Elliott! You just wanted me to say it first!" She shoved at my chest, but I pulled her back in, laughing.

"Damn right, I did!" I lowered my lips to hers, even though I was still laughing. "I love you."

"You better for the stunt you just pulled."

I couldn't stop laughing.

Mostly because it was a surreal moment.

My daughter was safe. Nobody was going to take her from me.

And I'd gotten the girl. The one I'd lose—the one I never thought I'd see again.

But she was mine.

Peyton was mine.

I had the most incredible sense of peace settle over me, and I knew instantly, this was how my life was supposed to be.

Until the crash from the kitchen.

Peyton froze. "Did that sound like eggs to you?"

My eyes widened. "No. Did it to you?"

She nodded, grimacing.

"Uh-oh," Briony said from the kitchen. "Mimi, we donna need more edds."

Peyton shook before she pressed her face, again, into my chest, and laughed.

Yep.

This was how my life was supposed to be.

And I'd never been happier.

THE END

Thank you so much for reading The Hook-Up Experiment. I hope you enjoyed Peyton's story! Chloe's story, THE DATING EXPERIMENT, is coming May 8th, 2018, and is now available for pre-order across all retailers!

THE DATING EXPERIMENT

1.Get over my best friend's brother.
2.Remember that I'm over him.
3.Prove I can date other people.
It should be easy.
It's not.

Setting up a dating website with the guy I've been in love with since I was five wasn't my smartest idea.
Especially since he's my best friend's brother—thankfully, she's okay with the fact I'm pulling a Sandy and I'm hopelessly devoted to him.
Which is why it's time to get over him.
So I do something crazy and ask Dominic Austin to find me a date. He does—if I find him one, too.
Since we own Stupid Cupid, it should be easy, right?
And it is.
My date is perfect. His date is perfect. Everything is perfect.
Until he kisses me…

Three dates.
One kiss.
And a big-ass mess…

ABOUT THE AUTHOR

Emma Hart is the New York Times and USA TODAY bestselling author of over thirty novels and has been translated into several different languages.

She is a mother, wife, lover of wine, Pink Goddess, and valiant rescuer of wild baby hedgehogs.

Emma prides herself on her realistic, snarky smut, with comebacks that would make a PMS-ing teenage girl proud.

Yes, really. She's that sarcastic.

You can find her online at:
www.emmahart.org
www.facebook.com/emmahartbooks
www.instagram.com/EmmaHartAuthor
www.pinterest.com/authoremmahart

Alternatively, you can join her reader group at http://bit.ly/EmmaHartsHartbreakers.

You can also get all things Emma to your email inbox by signing up for Emma Alerts*. http://bit.ly/EmmaAlerts

*Emails sent for sales, new releases, pre-order availability, and cover reveals. Each cover reveal contains an exclusive excerpt.

BOOKS BY EMMA HART

The Vegas Nights series:
Sin
Lust

Stripped series:
Stripped Bare
Stripped Down

The Burke Brothers:
Dirty Secret
Dirty Past
Dirty Lies
Dirty Tricks
Dirty Little Rendezvous

The Holly Woods Files:
Twisted Bond
Tangled Bond
Tethered Bond
Tied Bond
Twirled Bond
Burning Bond
Twined Bond

By His Game series:
Blindsided
Sidelined
Intercepted

Call series:
Late Call
Final Call
His Call

Wild series:
Wild Attraction
Wild Temptation
Wild Addiction
Wild: The Complete Series

The Game series:
The Love Game
Playing for Keeps
The Right Moves
Worth the Risk

Memories series:
Never Forget
Always Remember

Standalones:
Blind Date
Being Brooke
Catching Carly
Casanova
Mixed Up
Miss Fix-It
Miss Mechanic
The Upside to Being Single
The Hook-Up Experiment
The Dating Experiment (coming May 8, 2018)
Four Day Fling (coming July 24th)